DIANA MARS
PERIL IN PARADISE

SILHOUETTE *Desire*
Published by Silhouette Books
America's Publisher of Contemporary Romance

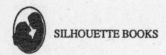

SILHOUETTE BOOKS

ISBN 0-373-05906-X

PERIL IN PARADISE

DIANA MARS

feels fortunate to be a part of the Golden Age of Romance, which has seen so many exciting elements added: suspense, horror, mystery, the supernatural. Although she has worked in the fields of business, languages and anthropology, writing has proven to be the strongest, yet most satisfying, challenge.

To my mother—
who continues to believe

One

Preston Kilpatrick tripped over a tree root and fell flat on his face. As soon as he got to his feet, a swarm of kissing bugs attacked him, and he began slapping at himself for all he was worth.

Beginning to feel dizzy from the self-inflicted blows that had connected with his face and neck, he ceased the flagellation.

Paradise Island, indeed!

The instant he stopped flailing his arms at the pesky, biting critters, they descended on him en masse. With an imaginative litany of curses, Preston skipped over several dead logs, and dived headfirst into what he took to be an inviting pond.

The pond was only a few feet deep, and Preston's head immediately erupted into one large, swollen lump. Tears swam in his eyes as he staggered to his feet, dazed and disoriented.

Looking down, Preston saw a couple of black leaves against the golden brown of his calves. Swatting at them did not remove them from his legs, and in dawning horror, Preston realized they were leeches.

Yikes!

Launching himself out of the blue-green, freshwater pond, Preston began to run, racing as fast as he had twenty years ago, when he'd been the star of his high school track team.

Clementine Cahill and her mother, Celeste, were traversing a so-called nature trail and having one of their frequent arguments, when they heard a blood-curdling scream and saw a large blur speed by them.

A human voice, hoarse and terrified, was attached to the long, bronzed legs revealed by brief red shorts, and the naked, muscular torso, which gleamed from health and sweat under the torrid January sun.

Celeste, who considered herself an excellent judge of male flesh and prided herself on her twenty-twenty vision, noticed that the large hand which had swung inches from her nose had no wedding ring.

"Hurry, Clemmie! You've got to help that poor man."

"But Mom, he's yelling like a banshee. We don't know if he's dangerous—"

"Don't stand there arguing! You told me you *teach* self-defense at the community center. You can take care of yourself." With a mighty shove that belied her diminutive stature, Celeste sent her tall daughter in the direction of the man who'd streaked by. "Go! You can't let a human being suffer like that."

Clementine bit back her words of protest and took off after the stranger. Boy, could he run! She thought she was fast, but this man's speed was world-class.

Privately thinking the man was a loony-tunes who'd forgotten his straitjacket at the hotel, she decided to exercise the caution her mother lacked. Clementine might be a private detective and an expert at self-defense, but from the little she'd seen of the human missile as he shot past, he had looked at least a half-foot taller than her own five-ten, and he easily out-weighed her by fifty pounds.

Clementine was not a coward. Neither was she stupid nor a casual risk taker. The gambling genes belonged to her mother.

Despite all her tongue-hanging efforts to catch up with him, Clementine was not able to reach the screaming madman until he'd arrived at the resort. Several concerned guests of the Puerco Loco had gathered around the man, who, judging by the smooth baritone holding forth in colorful expletives of the King's English, was in some pain.

With a commanding tone, Clementine began to shove the curious onlookers aside, and immediately determined what had spooked the man.

Leeches!

Swallowing a grin, Clementine asked for a lighter from the growing number of gathered guests, and soon disposed of the problem.

Kneeling at the man's feet, Clementine had her face in proximity to the front of his shorts. She noticed the snug fit of the red material had become tighter.

Raising her gaze slowly past a small waist, impressive chest and massive shoulders, Clementine stopped at the man's cheeks. A wave of red suffused the stubble-darkened jaw.

A man blushing! What an unusual sight! Clementine's bow-shaped mouth began curving into a smile, but it froze in place as her gaze reached a pair of steel gray eyes. They were made darker by the frown surrounding them.

"Thank you, Ms.—" The man held out his hand to help her up, but Clementine ignored it, straightening in one fluid movement.

"Cahill," Clementine supplied as she looked for the owner of the gold lighter.

"Muchas gracias," she told the distinguished-looking gentleman, handing him his lighter.

As the Spaniard came forward to retrieve the lighter, complimenting her quick actions in Spanish, Clementine missed the two men who had just emerged from the hotel. The taller, fairer of the two pulled his companion back into the entryway.

Preston noticed the furtive movements near the front lobby, but could not make out the two men who had melted into the shadows. Knowing that if he made any dramatic efforts to reach the hotel through this minimob, he could blow his cover—if, indeed, those two individuals were involved in anything more nefarious than wanting to keep out of the hot sun—Preston decided to bide his time.

As his savior turned her attention back to him, Preston forced a smile. "I'd like to thank you for what you did. It's a bit embarrassing for a grown man to be—"

"Disgusted?" Clementine quickly supplied. "I know the feeling. While other people are afraid of poisonous snakes or spiders, my nemesis is the cockroach. I know they don't bite, but I hate the ugly, pestilence-carrying, slimy flattops. Fear doesn't enter into the equation, just a profound loathing and revulsion. You might even say pathological aversion.''

The remaining frost melted from the man's eyes, and they now gleamed like antique silver. Clementine's very fit heart skipped a beat at the grin that flashed even white teeth.

"Pathological aversion. Exactly. You hit the nail on the head.'' Looking down at his scratched torso and legs, he added, "How lucky you happened to be here.''

Clementine did not correct him. It wouldn't help the man's already battered male ego to know that aid had only been yards away—had he noticed her running after him.

"It was nothing,'' Clementine dismissed lightly as she gathered her blue water jug and small canvas bag, which she'd dropped to the ground. Turning on her heel, she told him, "Better take care of those scratches. The tropics can wreak havoc on the immune system.''

Preston watched Clementine walk away with warring emotions.

What a woman!

Her tall, curvaceous figure filled out the turquoise tank top and white shorts to perfection. A riotous copper mane was barely contained with a multicolored scarf, and rested halfway down her bare back.

And what a back! Luscious shoulders, small waist, generous hips, heart-shaped buns, trim legs . . .

He shook his head to clear it, feeling that uncomfortable swelling in his groin once again. How could he have the hots for a woman he'd just met? It must be the infernal sun and the tumbles he'd taken. But what a woman!

And there was no doubt that she was all woman! He'd seen no shyness in her light gaze when she'd discovered his "condition"—rather, he'd noted a sense of knowledge and recognition and a certain amusement, which she had quickly veiled.

Preston groaned. Of all the lousy luck!

Here he was following a lead an investigative reporter pal of his from Miami had given him about a possible divorce racket and he had to meet the woman of his dreams.

Further complicating matters, his uncle was divorcing Delores—a woman Preston loved to hate, and who he suspected was a lot brainier than she let on—and the two birds in one stone Preston had hoped to kill were turning out to be turkeys.

How on earth could he keep his reporter status under wraps while conducting an investigation—making sure Uncle Ford did not become involved in anything shady or sinister—and still court the long-legged knockout who'd twisted his insides into pretzels?

To top it off, she had seen him at his worst.

She must think he was a sniveling coward!

Shaking his head at the cruel humor of the gods, Preston reassured the few remaining guests that he was okay and headed for the small drugstore located near the resort's pro shop.

With his luck, if he didn't disinfect his myriad bites and scratches, he'd end up with the bubonic plague.

* * *

What Preston didn't notice was two shadowy figures watching Clementine depart to find her mother, and Preston stride in the direction of the pro shop.

"Damn!" said the fair-haired man, detaching himself from the protective darkness outside the main lobby door. Turning to his companion, who was looking at him with a worried frown on his leathery face, he exclaimed, "Do you know who that is?"

The shorter man shook his head, his gaze alternating from Clementine's to Preston's departing forms. "Trouble?" he hazarded, removing a Cuban cigar from the pocket of his Western shirt.

"With a capital T," the tall man said. Making sure the coast was clear, he quickly went down the front steps, and added over his shoulder, "Come on. We've got work to do."

Two

"What time are you and Ronald appearing before the judge?"

"Oh, we're not due until the day after tomorrow," Celeste said.

Clementine paused in the act of putting star-shaped earrings on her pierced ears. The tiny diamonds and sapphires blinked in the sunlight streaming through the French windows of the *casita*.

"What do you mean, day after tomorrow? Why did you insist on having me drop everything to hold your hand? As if you've ever needed your hand held in your entire life."

"Now, Clemmie," Celeste said soothingly. "You know I'm a romantic at heart. I consider hand-holding quite touching . . . literally."

Clementine snorted inelegantly.

"You know what I mean." Tightening the white belt cinching her narrow waist, Clementine added accusingly, "First you tell me that Ronald has changed lately, gone most of the time, and you managed to sound so lost and forlorn—"

"That's true," Celeste agreed, smoothing the folds of a short coral dress, which showed off her slim, petite figure to great advantage. "I had a hard time even pinning him down on a date for our 'happy divorce.' He was totally opposed to divorcing in the first place. And even though it was my idea, it's still a hard thing to go through."

Celeste slid on ridiculously high high-heeled strap sandals, which increased her height to average. She had the legs and balance of Tina Turner, Clementine thought rather enviously, while she herself had to be careful not to trip on modest two-inchers.

She sighed. It continuously amazed her that not only were she and Celeste related, they were mother and daughter. The light blue eyes were one of the few traits she'd inherited from her mother—the sky hue was a very stubborn gene in the Forrester family tree. Her height and auburn hair she'd gotten from the Cahill side . . . along with her sense of independence, lack of pretension and appreciation of the simple life.

As Celeste put on several gold bracelets and an impressive Rolex, Clementine sighed again at their very ingrained differences. She would not even own a piece of jewelry were it not for her mother's generous gifts showered on her at every conceivable opportunity: birthdays, Christmas, Easter, and any other appropriate—or inappropriate—holiday.

Celeste must have noticed her daughter's downbeat expression, because she came over and put her arm around Clementine's shoulders—an astounding feat in itself, considering the older woman's small stature.

"Come on, Tweetie," Celeste chided. "Here you are on a beautiful island which has at least one attractive possibility... and all you do is complain about your poor mother?"

Clementine continued to pout, but she knew she could not hold out for long. Her mother's charm and joie de vivre were legendary.

"Look around... Isn't this a wonderful place?"

Clementine had to agree. Although not up to the luxurious standards Celeste was used to, the *casita* was large and airy, with a breathtaking view of the ocean. It also had the advantage of a super-large bathtub, where she could stretch out without having to tuck her knees under her chin.

"It's all right, I guess," Clementine conceded with careful enthusiasm. She gently disengaged herself from her mother's embrace, before Celeste popped a shoulder socket out of joint. As it was, Celeste gingerly rubbed her sore arm as she lowered it, and Clementine hid a smile.

Smoothing the full skirt of her navy blue dress, Clementine said, "But that still doesn't excuse your tricking me into dropping everything to come with you."

"Sweetheart, look in the mirror," Celeste said, her tone uncharacteristically somber. "Just look at those dark circles, and the lines around your mouth... You're overworked, and if you don't take any time off, you're not going to do yourself or your clients any good." Her voice a mixture of soft bitterness and reminiscence, Celeste added, "You know I'm a creature who needs a lot of attention, sweetheart. And you remind me so much of your dad—that damn man also worked too hard—''

Amazingly, Celeste, the very essence of self-control, turned away from Clementine and went to get her purse, a white straw monstrosity that contained anything anyone could ever need in any kind of emergency. Worried about the crack in her mother's voice, Clementine took a quick step toward her, but Celeste turned to face her, her cloak of equanimity restored.

"I just want you to enjoy life, sweetheart, before it's too late. Your father and I might never have divorced had he paid more attention to you and me. . . .''

Suddenly catching herself being serious—something Celeste always tried to avoid—she gave a self-deprecating grin and shrugged her shoulders.

"But heck, who am I to complain? Here I am about to be divorced for the second time—guess that means I'm the one at fault, right?''

Clementine was surprised at her mother's body language. Could that be uncertainty she read? Crossing the room in three quick strides, Clementine threw her arms around Celeste and gave her a fierce hug.

"Of course you're not totally at fault. I love Dad dearly, but he *is* a workaholic.'' Stepping back and looking her mother in the eye, Clementine added, "He deserted me, too, don't forget. And yet you made sure the divorce was not acrimonious. And you constantly reminded me as I was growing up just how much Dad really loved me. . . .''

Celeste gave Clementine a tremulous smile, and surreptitiously wiped at a little wetness at the corner of her beautifully made-up eye. "As for Ronald,'' Clementine added with undisguised distaste, "I always said he wasn't good enough for you.''

Celeste gave Clementine a brief, hard hug. "Come on, let's go. I'm famished."

With a last pat at her perfect coiffure, Celeste blew out of the room in a cloud of expensive floral perfume.

Clementine's lips parted in a smile that was partly affectionate, partly exasperated. She picked up her matching navy-and-white clutch and both room keys, turned off the television set, which always blared in any space Celeste occupied, and followed her mother at a more leisurely pace.

In the hotel dining room, Celeste and Clementine decided against partaking of the buffet, which took up almost one wall of the large, sun-drenched room. Because the island had once belonged to Argentina, then had been taken over in succession by England, Brazil and now Uruguay, a variety of dishes were represented. Foremost among them was the South American *asado,* or barbecue, of Argentinean beef, one of the most tender in the world.

Although South Americans did not typically eat steak at breakfast, a version of steak and eggs had been included in the buffet for the many gringos patronizing the resort. Since neither Clementine nor Celeste liked to see plain beef before lunchtime, they decided to have something from the menu instead of the buffet. Celeste ordered over-easy eggs, bacon, sausage, puffy *papas fritas* and fresh *pan frances,* while Clementine chose *panqueques* with *dulce de leche,* an Argentinean delicacy of milk jelly liberally lathered on pancakes. After much internal debate, Clementine also decided on a side order of bacon, one of her greater weaknesses. While Celeste could eat everything in sight and still keep her svelte figure without raising a sweat, the only way Clementine could keep her figure was by committing to an exercise program.

"Well, at least you can't complain about the food," Celeste was saying minutes later as the small table they were occupying threatened to overflow with her selections.

"The food is excellent, but it's lucky I didn't order anything else or I'd be eating from the floor," Clementine said as she savored the fatty, rich flavor of the thick, crisp bacon, which, like everything else, was grilled.

Celeste dismissed her daughter's complaint with an airy wave of her hand. Her equilibrium had been completely restored, and dining well would put Celeste in a happy mood for the rest of the day. "I've told you often enough, Tweetie, you don't eat enough to feed a bird. And with your Junoesque proportions, you need to fuel the furnace or you'll—"

Clementine looked up as Celeste ceased one of her favorite lectures, the one entitled One hundred and One Reasons You Should Eat More, and followed the line of her mother's gaze.

Waiting to be seated in the crowded dining room was the man she had rescued yesterday.

The piece of pancake and gooey *dulce de leche* stuck in Clementine's throat as she suddenly divined her mother's intention. Clementine aimed for Celeste's arm, which was already up and waving, but missed as her mother adroitly outmaneuvered her, raising her other hand.

"Mother," Clementine began warningly, but it was too late.

The man saw Celeste, slid his gaze to her companion and recognition dawned in the deep gray eyes. With no hesitation, he made his way to their table.

"Good morning," he said to both women, but his appreciative glance rested on Clementine.

Clementine was sure she could hear the wheels rattling in her mother's head, and tried to head her off at the pass.

"How nice to see you again," Clementine said, getting up. "And how lucky for you. The room is so crowded, and here I was just leaving. Why don't you sit down and keep my mother company?"

"Nonsense," Celeste said sweetly, grabbing her daughter's belt and giving a vicious tug. Clementine found herself unceremoniously slammed back down into her seat. She felt the wave of mortified pink tingeing her cheeks change to a flaming red at the man's smothered grin. "This young man doesn't want to be saddled with an old lady for company. You know you always like to have a second cup of coffee after you finish eating."

While that much was true, wild horses wouldn't drag the admission from Clementine at this moment. "You know I am trying to cut down on caffeine," she told her mother through a smile covering gritted teeth. "I have trouble falling asleep at night."

"That's because you're overworked, darling. You were really due for a vacation," Celeste said with motherly concern, all the while eyeing the handsome man. "Please sit down," she invited him. "And tell us how you feel after your ordeal yesterday."

To his credit, the man remained standing and with admirable sensitivity—or was it the sixth sense of feeling a trap ready to spring?—he asked Clementine, "If you're sure I'm not intruding..."

"Of course not," Celeste answered for Clementine. "My daughter eats like a bird, and she's done. We have plenty of room."

Both Celeste and the man Clementine had rescued looked at her, the former threateningly, the latter politely. Glancing around the room, Clementine offered weakly, "The dining room seems filled to capacity. Please do join us."

Celeste smiled like the proverbial Cheshire cat while the man took an extra seat, apparently undaunted by Clementine's less than overwhelming enthusiasm. "Allow me to introduce myself. I'm Preston Kilpatrick."

"I'm Celeste Cahill, and this fast-thinking young woman is my daughter, Clementine."

Clementine noticed the quickly hidden grin that brought out two rugged dimples in the man's bronzed face. This whole thing was so embarrassing she was ready to slug someone, but since her mother was out of the question, Preston Kilpatrick made an excellent second choice.

"And how are you feeling, Mr. Kilpatrick?" Celeste asked again. Persistence was one of her fortes—ranking right behind unabashed audacity and impertinent inquisitiveness.

"Please call me Preston, Mrs. Cahill. None the worse for wear, thank you. Are you here to avail yourselves of the 'happy divorce'?"

"I am," Celeste said quickly. "From my second husband. Clementine has never been married."

Clementine was mortified, but thankfully Preston ignored Celeste's pointed comment. "You know, Mrs. Cahill, you really told a patent untruth just now."

As the waiter approached to take Preston's order, both women stared at him in fascination, Celeste because she had yet to be taken to task on any of her charming—or outrageous—white lies, and Clementine because she was curious to find out which of her mother's meddlesome schemes a relative stranger could have uncovered already.

"You are certainly *not* an old lady, Mrs. Cahill—"

"Celeste, please."

"Because not only are you gorgeous, you cannot be much older than I." Celeste breathed easier and gave him one of her high-watt smiles.

What Preston said was obviously true, if somewhat saccharine. With her perfect figure, pert blond hairdo and virtually unlined peaches'n'cream complexion, Celeste truly *looked* to be about Preston's age, late thirties, just a few years older than Clementine's thirty-one years. Celeste had graduated from a private school at sixteen, and had met Sterling Cahill her first year in college. She'd married him at seventeen, despite loud family protests. Clementine had arrived shortly thereafter.

So the perfect complexion that belied Celeste's true age—another Forrester trait Clementine fortunately *had* inherited—owed nothing to cosmetic surgery and a lot to blessed heredity and vigilance against aging effects of the sun's rays.

"How nice of you to say so. But I know you'll enjoy yourself much more with a contemporary like my daughter." Clementine felt like one of the steers on display at Chicago's famed meat blocks. Ignoring

Clementine's daggerlike looks, Celeste said, beaming, "You know, not only is Clementine beautiful, but she is also an accomplished athlete and career woman." Clementine kicked her mother under the table, terrified of what was coming next. But there was no stopping the maternal juggernaut. "Speaking of athleticism, my daughter was a track and tennis star in college, but she was not able to catch up with you yesterday. You really *are* fast, aren't you?"

Preston choked on the coffee he'd just sipped. "Catch up with me?"

Clementine tried to anticipate her mother, but once again Celeste beat her to the punch. "Yep, a regular Speedy Gonzalez. Didn't you notice Clemmie here giving you chase? But of course, you were making so much noise tramping through the bushes, you probably didn't hear her when she was trying to get you to stop so she could help you."

Clementine closed her eyes. Suddenly, she knew how the Titanic passengers felt as the ship hit the iceberg.

Preston said in a strangled voice, "I must have sounded like a herd of elephants."

As Preston's accusing glance met Clementine's, she felt lower than an earthworm. He must be thinking she'd had a good laugh at his expense.

"And you screamed like a banshee," Celeste agreed, for once not picking up on the bad vibes. "At first, Clemmie was reluctant to go after you.... She was afraid you might be unstable or even dangerous."

When Preston's sensual mouth thinned, Clementine knew he did not merely suspect her of having had fun at his expense. He was thoroughly convinced. And no doubt he considered both Cahill women to be unstable and dangerous.

Feeling reduced to the size of a Smurf despite her generous proportions, Clementine felt sorry for Preston. Her mother had not known that Clementine had tried to spare Preston's feelings by not telling him the whole story yesterday, and now his male ego must be smarting more intensely than his physical wounds.

Polar coolness had invaded Preston's eyes and tone when he addressed Clementine. "Who can blame you? One can't be too careful nowadays, and I must have looked ridiculous, a grown man acting in such an... undignified manner."

It had apparently dawned on Celeste that diplomatic relations had ceased around the table. Looking from her daughter's pained expression to Preston's icy visage, Celeste tried spin control to minimize damage.

"As you so reasonably pointed out, Preston, an attractive young woman cannot be too careful in today's violent world." Clementine turned to her mother, mouth agape, remembering full well whose idea it had been to help the "poor man" in the first place. Blithely ignoring the indignation and accusation in Clementine's eyes, Celeste continued, "But she must have found you sane and capable, because she didn't say anything else about you after she helped you out."

"I must have made quite an impression," Preston said dryly.

"Nonsense," Celeste said smartly. "My daughter likes you, I can tell."

"Mother!" Clementine said, enraged.

"Despite my many shortcomings?" Preston asked, left eyebrow raised in disbelief.

"Who's perfect?" Celeste asked.

Clementine clenched her teeth against an urge to recite a litany of Celeste Cahill imperfections.

"If you'll both excuse me, I have some phone calls to make," Clementine said.

"I thought we had agreed you were going to concentrate on having fun," Celeste said, not hiding her displeasure.

Feeling the last of her willpower evaporating, Clementine managed to say in an even tone, "I have several things hanging in the air, as you well know. Petey needs some help back home–"

"Go, go!" Celeste said, waving her off. Clementine knew that although her mother was supportive of her choice of profession, she worried about her, not only because being a private detective was a dangerous way to make a living, but also because she thought it would intimidate a potential suitor. Celeste obviously did not want to scare Preston off—although Clementine suspected the damage had been done already—and cut her daughter off before Clementine could reveal she was a private investigator. "Clemmie is such a dedicated, hardworking businesswoman. Very reliable and dependable."

Now Celeste was making her sound like a Hoover appliance. What had gotten into her mother today? She wasn't usually so heavy-handed.

As Clementine excused herself, Preston rose, too, and their eyes met. His gaze was unreadable, and she could hardly blame him. Men—and many women—for that matter, disliked matchmaking tactics. And

Celeste's revelations about yesterday had done nothing to smooth the waters.

Clementine shook her head as she slowly left the table and made her way to her room, puzzled anew at her mother's lack of subtlety. Deciding to work off her breakfast *and* mortification before settling in for some serious phoneconferencing, Clementine retraced her steps to the dining room and was about to head for one of the walking paths behind the hotel when she saw a man standing by Celeste's table. The tilt of his head and broad build looked familiar, as did the proud carriage, but Clementine immediately put any concern out of her mind.

She had enough on her plate right now without adding worry about a potential beau of her mother's.

Three

Looking down at her low-heeled sandals, Clementine ruefully reflected that she should have changed her shoes before embarking on this little walk. Even though she had chosen the nature trail marked Paseo Fácil—the "easy trail"—her constitutional had turned into a trek when she'd adventuresomely taken a fork in the road.

Well, she had no one but herself to blame for letting her mother get to her or for lacking the foresight to change footgear. As she stooped to remove some pebbles that had become embedded in her skin, she heard male voices whispering. While the presence of other people wasn't so unusual—she'd met other nature walkers from the hotel on the trail—years in the business had taught Clementine that when someone whispered in such an innocuous setting, that person was hiding something.

Cursing the attire that had been appropriate for an elegant dining room but was unsuitable for a little surveillance, Clementine tried to gather her full skirt around her legs and stood sideways behind a tree. Unfortunately, her bust dimensions were of the peak rather than valley variety, and she was afraid they would be noticed in short order.

Crouching low, trying to blend into a prickly *ombú* bush, Clementine heard a few words that set her teeth on edge.

"—easy marks. No, no, don't worry about it. I don't think...suspects."

The second voice had a lower octave, so Clementine was not able to make out the words.

"Hey, what passes for law around here won't give us any trouble...don't worry."

Apparently, one party was either paranoid or a good planner, because the other man insisted, "No, I tell you. No one saw me take this path from the Puerco Loco."

Clementine frowned. The Puerco Loco? Thieves, con men, maybe even worse...operating from the resort?

She heard the other man say something indistinctly to his louder companion. The rustling of paper followed. A payoff? Incriminating evidence being bought? Drugs changing hands?

And then heavy footsteps were coming her way.

Damning her luck, Clementine dropped to the ground and felt rocks, insects and prickly leaves dig into her low-cut halter top. She cursed silently. One of her few expensive outfits, down the drain.

Biting her lips against the pain of numerous hungry insects feasting on her skin, Clementine waited until the man walked by, then got up slowly and silently.

After verifying that both men were heading in separate directions, Clementine began tailing the one who was taking the path back to the Puerco Loco.

By the time Clementine emerged from the dense jungle growth, she saw a tall man dressed in white go into the hotel. The sun glinted on his silver-blond hair. Clementine broke into a trot, but he was nowhere to be seen when she entered the main lobby. She asked a bellhop and the desk clerk if they'd seen anything, but both said no. Clementine stamped her foot in frustration.

As she turned on her heel and wobbled back toward her room, Preston and an older man stepped into the lobby—the same one who had been standing by her mother's table earlier that morning.

Now Clementine could see why the man had looked familiar: almost as tall as Preston, he had the same erect posture, athletic build and silver-gold hair. His eyes, unlike Preston's, were dark blue, and they were regarding her curiously.

And he was dressed in white.

Shock registered in both Clementine's and Preston's eyes at the same moment. But for very different reasons.

"Hell's bells, young lady, what happened to you?" the older man asked.

Clementine's startled gaze slid from Preston to the stranger, and she missed the look of concern on Preston's face.

"I fell in the bushes," she said shortly. Had this been the man she'd been following?

"You? Fall in the bushes?" Preston's disbelieving snort did not help matters. "And after I've just been treated to a blow-by-blow account of your athletic prowess."

Clementine winced inwardly at the mental picture his words conjured. "I tripped. I made the mistake of taking a walk in these," Clementine said, ignoring his sarcasm and pointing to her scuffed sandals. "And those paths are really treacherous."

The moment the words were out, Clementine could have kicked herself. Not only was it clear that Preston wasn't buying any of it, but on top of everything, she had just informed the older man, possibly a criminal, that she *might* have traipsed over the same path he had.

The older man's eyes showed an alert interest, but Clementine could read nothing else in them. Of course, that held no great significance, because con men and hardened criminals—the successful ones— were notorious for their poker faces. They could also seem perfectly normal and helpful, hiding their sociopathic tendencies behind a totally innocent facade.

Eyes narrowed, Preston told Clementine, "This divorce deal on an advertised paradise island is claiming quite a few victims." Grabbing her arm, he began to steer her out of the lobby. "You'd better get those cuts and bites treated."

The urgency in Preston's voice seeped into her brain...but could she trust him? After all, he was a perfect stranger. In the company of the man who could very well be one of the two suspicious characters she'd overheard.

Digging in her heels and shaking off Preston's hold, Clementine said, "You haven't introduced me to your...companion."

"I'd like to apologize for my nephew's unfortunate lapse in manners. Let me assure you it is only a temporary aberration. He is normally a very decent, engaging fellow." Extending an immaculately manicured hand, the man smiled and added, "I'm Rutherford Kilpatrick. And please, call me Ford."

Against her better judgment, Clementine smiled back. Preston's uncle—if that was his true identity— was a real charmer.

"Clementine Cahill." She shook Ford's hand firmly, and liked the strong pressure he exerted. Strong, but not overpowering *or* wimpy. Clementine put a lot of stock into handshakes, and the ones she distrusted the most were the weak kind, the ones that had the consistency of soggy spaghetti.

"Ah, the enchanting daughter of an equally engaging woman, the lovely Celeste," Ford said in a smooth baritone, very much like Preston's.

Could his have been the voice Clementine had heard in the clearing?

"You've met my mother, then?" Clementine asked, wanting to find out how long he'd remained at the table. "Were you also regaled with tales of my exploits, just as poor Preston was?"

"Unfortunately, no. I, too, am here for a divorce, and I had to take care of some details."

That explained his reason for being on Isla Gaucha. At least, his purported one. But what was Preston doing here?

Clementine looked at him, waiting to see if he was going to offer a reason for his being on the island, too. But he merely stared back at her with an enigmatic smile.

"Well, that's what I have to do, too," Clementine said crisply. "Take care of some details."

"Would you like some help?" Preston offered. "After all, turnabout is fair play."

"Thanks. But mother carries a first-aid kit with her. She can help me out."

Clementine could not wait to leave and ask her assistant back in the States to fax her any information he could find on Preston and Rutherford Kilpatrick. Were they really nephew and uncle? Con men? Or both?

In a complete non sequitur, she asked Ford, "Did you say you knew my mother from Denver?"

Both men looked at each other, then at her. Let them think her brains were addled because of her fall.

Polite to the end, Ford answered, "No, I'd never met your mother before today. We're from California."

That explained the fabulous tan and great body, Clementine thought, openly admiring Preston's physique. Then, realizing she may be showing more than professional detachment, she told herself to stop looking at the magnificent shoulders and chest so lovingly covered by a black T-shirt, and concentrate on probing further.

Trying to lead him on, she said to Preston, "You must have gotten that tan in San Diego." The admiring tinge to her voice was not faked.

"As a matter of fact, we're from San Francisco." From the way Preston was looking at her, Clementine could tell he was convinced she was in need of *serious* help.

Not wanting to attract any more suspicion, she smiled and said, "I'd better get these bites and scratches taken care of. Nice meeting you, Ford."

Clementine could feel both men's puzzled glances boring into her back as she walked out of the lobby.

She just hoped she had not given herself away to Ford. Or Preston... if he was also involved.

In any case, within a few hours, she would be in a position to make a more educated guess. Peter Danforth, her assistant who was studying criminology and hoped to become a private eye, was quick and efficient. He would ferret out anything significant regarding the Kilpatricks, and would be able to tell her if either of them had a rap sheet.

It surprised her how strong her hope was that Preston Kilpatrick didn't have one.

The short man with the weathered face grinned as he watched Clementine depart, settling more comfortably into the plush couch of the lobby.

The boss had been right when he'd written those brief instructions in the notebook he always carried:

Someone's listening. I'll play decoy. You follow listener.

An organized man, his boss. Organized and dangerous. The boss had noticed someone hiding in the bushes even as he was interrogating the hell out of him.

Making it so easy to be tailed to the hotel was also a stroke of genius. While the good-looking broad had almost killed herself in those dainty heels as she followed a white suit, he'd been able to shadow her.

And she didn't suspect a thing.

"You never mentioned how attractive Clementine was, Preston," Ford told his nephew as they watched her leave.

Preston shrugged his wide shoulders. "This resort is full of good-looking women."

Ford looked at Preston shrewdly. "Don't give me that bull. There might be other attractive women here, but none with her intelligence and personality."

"You could tell all that from our brief, strange conversation?" Preston asked as he headed for the door.

Ford followed his nephew outside. "I can read between the lines. When you act unimpressed, that's when I know you're hooked."

"I'm not hooked—" Preston stopped midsentence and shook his head when he saw his uncle's grin. "You old son of a—" Quickly changing the subject, he asked, "When is Delores arriving?"

"She phoned me yesterday, and said she'd be getting in tonight, around seven. She's taking the hydroplane from Montevideo."

"Good luck to Delores," Preston murmured with nasty glee. A storm had been predicted for tonight, and he wished her nothing but stormy skies and choppy waters.

"I heard that," Ford warned him. "I know you're not crazy about Delores, but there's no need to wish her any ill. And no reason that she and I end our marriage on an acrimonious note."

"As long as she doesn't get you to change your mind again, I'll have nothing but best wishes for her."

"You're too hard on Delores. She likes money, but she's basically good-hearted, and fun and exciting to be around."

"So are barracuda. And speaking of fun, Uncle, what about Celeste..."

"Please. I came here to be divorced, not to pick up another playmate—a role which would not fit Celeste, in any case. Don't play matchmaker, Preston. The part doesn't suit you."

"As long as it gets you away from Delores, I'll play any role."

"What was that?" Ford asked, hurrying after Preston.

Preston ignored him and ordered a taxi. He needed to get into town and meet with the contact his friend in Miami had arranged. Tony Esperanza had advised that he get a gun, since some of the rumors that had gotten back to the States indicated a dangerous mastermind was involved, not only in the divorce racket, but other schemes, as well.

Above all, Preston wanted to make sure his uncle didn't fall into any nasty criminal web. Ford might be a pain in the butt sometimes, but Preston loved his father's younger—and only—brother dearly. And he knew the affection was just as strongly returned.

Preston knew Ford did not intend to heed his nephew's warning. He was going to have to keep an eye on his uncle, and make damn sure he was prepared if and when the need arose.

Back in her hotel room, Clementine called her office. "Peter, I need you to do a criminal and civil background check on two men. They claim to be uncle and nephew. Rutherford and Preston Kilpatrick. They are both over six feet, with muscular builds. Uncle is about fifty, nephew in his late thirties.''

She waited while Peter took everything down. "I thought you were going to South America to relax, boss," Peter chided her gently.

"You know how it is, Petey. I find mysteries in everything."

Peter chuckled and asked. "Any identifying characteristics? Driver's license or social security numbers?''

"Just became acquainted, Peter. If you run dry, I'll break into their suites. For now, no visibles. Both uncle and nephew have light blond hair. Ford has blue eyes, Preston's are dark gray. Preston also has a wide forehead, square jaw, Roman blade of a nose, high prominent cheekbones, long dark lashes. They say they're from San Francisco.''

Clementine checked herself as she heard the loud silence on the line. "Go on, boss. Please carry on."

She gulped, and heard the sound magnified over the wires. She could also hear Peter's contained chuckle, and felt herself turn hot all over.

"Ah, that's about it, Petey. Just fax me the info as soon as you have it, will you?''

"Imidiatamundo," Petey said smartly.

Chuckling, Clementine corrected, "That's *inmediatamente,* you silly fool."

Petey added solemnly, "I won't let you down, boss, because this Preston guy sounds like a real desperado. Was that one or two scars on his high prominent cheekbones?''

"Oh, shut up, you smart aleck," Clementine snapped. "Just do your job. And put me up to date on the rest of the cases."

"Yes, ma'am," Peter said, and proceeded as ordered. Once he'd filled Clementine in, he added, "And boss—"

"Yes, Petey?"

"Please be careful with this long-lashed Kilpatrick dude. He might—"

"Goodbye, Peter," Clementine said before slamming down the phone.

Four

An hour later, after a nice hot shower and a painful session with alcohol and hydrogen peroxide, Clementine left her room to look for her mother.

The clerk at the front desk hadn't seen Celeste, and a search of the hotel, rec rooms, restaurants, bars, hotel grounds, the pool, tennis courts and game room still didn't produce her mother.

Gustavo, a waiter, was finally able to tell Clementine that he'd seen Celeste hitch a ride with a young couple who were going to the beach for scuba diving lessons.

Wondering if her mother was going to try skydiving or mountain climbing next, Clementine asked Gustavo if he knew where Preston Kilpatrick had gone.

"Oh, yes, *señorita*. Señor Kilpatrick and his uncle went into town."

Clementine's antennae prickled.

"Into town?"

"Yes, while Señor Kilpatrick was waiting for a taxi, I overheard him tell his uncle that he needed to dig up some information."

Clementine frowned. Information? Of course, he *could* be a historian, researching the rich culture and folklore of the region. But somehow Clementine did not think so. As a woman in what was still regarded a man's profession, she knew better than to pigeonhole people into occupations based solely on their gender or looks. And she'd seen too many out-of-shape detectives and weight-lifting professors to trust stereotypes. Besides, Preston struck her as a man of action, not someone who would willingly work a nine-to-five job.

Very much like her, who loathed desk work and loved to be out in the field.

But what information could he be digging up?

"*Señorita?* Señorita Cahill? Are you all right?"

Clementine looked blankly at Gustavo for a moment, then realized the young man was regarding her oddly.

She tended to go into a trance when the pieces to a puzzle did not immediately fall into place. Wanting to reassure Gustavo, she placed a hand on his arm, and said, "Yes, I'm fine, Gustavo. It's just that Mr. Kilpatrick borrowed my camera, and since I need it before I can go into town..."

"Oh, if that is all, *señorita,* I can easily fix that. We keep some extra cameras that we lend to our guests—"

"No! That is... I really need my own camera. I am a camera buff, you see, and only my own will do..."

Clementine finished off weakly, knowing Gustavo must think she was yet another weird *norteamericana*. "You see, Gustavo, I am taking a course in photography back home, and part of the assignment requires that I use this particular camera. So it's imperative that I catch up with Señor Kilpatrick. I don't suppose you know where he went..." she said hopefully.

Apparently, her little brainstorm had set Gustavo at ease. He reflected for a moment, and then told her, "Yes, I remember now. Señor Kilpatrick told the driver to first take them to a pet store his uncle wanted to visit, and then he wanted to know how to get to the Cantina Víbora."

"*Muchas gracias,* Gustavo. You've been a great help."

"*No hay por que,* Señorita Cahill."

About ready to go, Clementine turned back and said, "By the way, Gustavo, would you recommend a drugstore in town? I have some bites that need a strong antibiotic."

"*Sí, señorita.* The *apotecario* at the Farmacia Sarmiento is very good. He will be able to help you."

Clementine hoped so. She thanked the helpful waiter again, asked him to get her a taxi and tipped him generously.

The bank of taxis to the south of the hotel was currently empty, Gustavo told her moments later, so Clementine had a short wait. She rubbed her sore chest. Some of the insect bites were already stinging, and her skin felt on fire from those plants she'd crushed with her fall.

Rotating her shoulders, Clementine tried to get some relief from the burning itch that was now invading her back. She hoped none of the plants she'd fallen on were the South American version of poison ivy.

Knowing that part of her discomfort arose from her doubts about Preston—who had *seemed* guileless and helpless but who could have been putting on an act—Clementine told herself to stop letting her imagination run away with her. Hopefully, there would be a reasonable explanation for all her suspicions.

Forty-five minutes later, Clementine had even more reason to be both miserably itchy and very suspicious.

She'd arrived at the Cantina Víbora—the bar's sign boasted an evil-looking snake entwined to make out the title in its namesake's image—just in time to see Preston hand something over to a man, and receive a small package in return. She'd been chasing Preston all over town, and sure hoped this was his last stop.

The stranger's appearance was not reassuring. With a dirty bandanna on his forehead and black patch over his eye, the swarthy man looked like a character straight out of a pirate novel.

Having nobly postponed getting her medication from the local drugstore, Clementine was doing her best to keep from scratching her bites, while trying to avoid being noticed by Preston at the same time.

After his little transaction he left the Cantina Víbora to meet with a short, swarthy man who obviously had information to sell. Clementine, who had followed him, tried to edge closer, plastering her body to the wall of the building next to the seedy-looking bar and hiding behind some scraggly bushes by the entrance.

As one of the prickly branches found her leg and buried itself in it, Clementine swore under her breath. The flora of this place was going to be the death of her yet.

Writing down a description of the stoolie in her notebook, Clementine saw Preston slip some money to the man, who spoke with a southwestern twang. She realized with a start that the man she'd overheard in the clearing had also spoken with a Texan accent. Could they be the same man?

Texas was close to Mexico, the boundaries saw a lot of drug runners and other illegal border activities. Could there be a connection?

Clementine fervently hoped not.

Besides which, it had not looked as if Preston had planned to meet with this last unsavory-looking character. It had looked as if the man himself had sought out Preston.

Cursing the sound of traffic and the boisterous barflies and tourists for only allowing her to hear isolated words like *compound* and *take you,* Clementine recorded one last entry in her notebook. Then she followed Preston to a local restaurant called El Pescador Feliz, which featured smiling fish on its colorful banner. She watched as Preston joined Ford at a lace-covered table in the middle of the sunny, spacious room.

Wanting to hear what the two men were discussing, Clementine entered the restaurant. Before she could claim a booth in a secluded corner, she saw Preston turn around and fix her with a less than friendly stare.

"Hi. Are you lost?"

He'd made her! Clementine gulped. How long had he known she was tailing him?

Forcing a smile, Clementine said, "Hi. Just looking for my mother."

"She's not here, my dear," Ford said, patting the seat next to his. "But you're welcome to join us."

"Thank you, but I can't stay. I need to visit the pharmacy to get some medicine."

"You do look a bit flushed. Are you feeling all right?" Ford said, his tone concerned.

Clementine ignored Preston's knowing gaze, and said airily, "I guess the fall took more out of me than I realized."

"You should be careful, my dear. I'm waiting for my wife—soon to be ex—to come in on the next *avión*. In the meantime, I was looking at some pets..." Turning to Preston, Ford added, "But I think Preston has finished his business in town. He can escort you to the pharmacy and I'll wait here until he returns."

"You're right, Uncle. I'll not only help Ms. Cahill find a good pharmacist, I'll also accompany her to the hotel and make sure she's taken care of."

Not liking the sound of that, Clementine said, "I've already been recommended a drugstore, and then I have other business to attend to. I don't need an escort—"

"The drugstore it is, then," Preston said, getting up and going to her side. Putting an arm around her waist, he added, "Shall we go?"

Once outside in the heat, Clementine removed the smile from her face and Preston's hand from her waist.

"Thank you for your concern, Mr. Kilpatrick—"

"Please call me Preston."

"But I'll be all right."

Preston shook his head, his grin infuriating. "No dice. I'd like to know why you were following me all over town."

Clementine stalked off in the direction of the drugstore. "Your question doesn't deserve an answer."

Preston easily kept pace with her. "Because you have something to hide?"

Clementine stopped dead in her tracks and pivoted sharply to face him. Preston's gaze held an underlying glint of steel, and she knew she'd been right in not underestimating him.

"I don't know what you mean." As Clementine turned away from him and began walking again, absently rubbing the multitude of bites and scratches she'd sustained, she told herself to be careful. She couldn't just dial 911 if she was in trouble. There were at least two people involved in whatever was going on. If Preston was part of the ring—whatever their scheme—they could soon find out that she was a private investigator.

Unless Preston already knew?

The thought made her pause, and she stumbled. Preston's hand shot out to steady her, its pressure around her waist making her even warier. The man was strong—physically as well as mentally. It was not easy keeping a woman of her size upright so effortlessly.

What if they went through her mother to get to her?

Fear paralyzed Clementine, and she swayed. Preston's hold tightened, and he drew her to him, letting his body support hers.

Clementine looked into Preston's face and read raw desire there. Leaning into his warm strength, she decided to take advantage of his obvious attraction to her—at least until she could make sure her mother was safely off the island. Clementine would never forgive herself if her mother was injured—or worse—because of her daughter's nose for trouble.

Lowering her lashes to hide her aversion to this charade, Clementine said in a throaty voice, "Okay, so you found me out. Do you have to carry on so?"

Preston kept one arm around her waist, and raised her chin with a firm hand. "What do you mean?" he asked, frowning.

"I mean," she said, her voice scratchy from worry and disgust at her subterfuge, "it was obvious yesterday we were attracted to each other. Do you have to make me spell it out?"

Preston looked at her, puzzled. Then the light of awareness dawned in his gray eyes, silvering them. The pressure of his fingers on her face eased, and they cupped her cheek.

"You mean you were following me because you're attracted to me?"

Clementine closed her eyes and swallowed hard. She had never chased a man, and never would. If a man was not interested in her as she was, attracted by *all* that she was, she would never try to seduce him.

Even though it went against her grain, and against every belief she held dear, Clementine forced what she hoped was a seductive smile to her lips.

"Boy, you really want your pound of flesh for the leeches episode, don't you?"

Doubt and confusion were reflected in Preston's face. It was obvious that he was tempted to believe her declaration, but just as obvious that he was neither gullible nor egotistical.

Another attack of itching made Clementine shudder, and she instinctively tried to scratch her chest.

Preston's hand shot out, stopping her.

"Don't. You might get those infected. They look pretty nasty."

Breathing a sigh of relief that she had gotten a short reprieve from her Mata Hari role, Clementine said ruefully, "I guess both of us have become intimately acquainted with the local flora—and the experience has not agreed with us."

Preston smiled, a genuine smile that stole her breath. "I'd rather become intimately acquainted with the fauna on this island."

"Oh, you have a thing for animals?" Clementine asked as Preston kept a supporting arm around her waist and steered her in the direction of the Farmacia Sarmiento.

He chuckled. "No, just a tall redhead who's not very good at lying. And who's got me curious to find out why."

Startled, Clementine glanced at Preston, but his expression was unreadable. He guided her into the drugstore, seated her on a bench with carved scenes of gauchos and Indians locked in mortal combat and approached the counter.

Clementine finished applying the last of the cream the pharmacist had recommended and sighed with relief. Pure heaven! She didn't know what the foul-smelling liniment contained, and she didn't want to know. All that mattered to her at the moment were the results.

After a hot bath, a couple of aspirin and the horse cream, she felt almost human again. Ready to take on the world.

But first, she had to find her mother, in case it became necessary to get her off the island.

The phone rang and Clementine picked it up on her way out of her room.

Peter's voice was a welcome sound, and she quickly filled him in on recent events.

"I'm afraid that I still haven't gotten the information you needed, boss. The computer crashed during a power outage and I'll have to borrow Spencer's." Spencer was a former client, and the owner of the computer store adjacent to Chalice Investigations in a Denver mall. "While you've been luxuriating in tropical heat, we've had windchills of seventy below, and two feet of snow."

"My heart bleeds for you, Peter," Clementine told him, fear for her mother's safety adding an edge to her voice. "But you have to hurry. I have to know what's going on here, and I have to know right away. If there's any hint of danger to Mom, I'm getting her out of here, fast. So please see if you can get her a ticket off this island as soon as possible. In the meantime, I'm going to look for her. She hasn't come back yet."

"Sorry, boss. I was working on the Hamilton case. I didn't think this was that urgent."

Clementine sighed. "I know, Petey. It's not your fault. It's mine for being seen by Preston Kilpatrick—for actually following him in the first place. Who knows? Maybe this will turn out to be a false alarm. But I'd like to be prepared, just in case. I'd hate to think that poking into other people's business could have put Mom in jeopardy."

"Don't blame yourself, boss. That's what makes you such a great investigator—your instincts. You wouldn't even be second-guessing yourself if your mother wasn't there—and she's the one that conned you into taking this vacation in the first place. She's a lot safer with you there to protect her, in case anything funny's going on."

Any other time, Clementine would have been pleased at Peter's compliment and absolute confidence in her. Right now, though, she was too busy blaming herself to respond with a teasing rejoinder.

"Please work fast, Petey."

"Sure thing, boss."

Preston paused in reviewing his notes, and rubbed his hand over his eyes.

From the information he'd gathered—including some red herrings and some off-the-wall tips from squealers who'd say anything for a fast buck—Preston realized a lot more was going on at Isla Gaucha than sight-seeing and "happy" divorcing. Some other leisure activities like blackmail, extortion and smuggling seemed to be the order of the day, as well.

He had put out the word in town that he was looking for information, and possibly some action. Tony Esperanza's guy had provided him with a gun, as well as a warning. The warning concerned a gringo, known only as the "Iceman," who was rumored to head a crime ring with diversified interests, including fleecing unsuspecting *divorciantes*. No one knew his identity, but everyone was convinced the man was ruthless, real bad news. Several stool pigeons had disappeared in the past few months, and the rest of the informants on the island were wary. They would not trust a new-comer, particularly a *norteamericano*.

Preston did not have to be told to be careful about information he had to pay for—especially from the furtive, shady characters he'd dealt with today. He knew that the data chain was fraught with hazards, and often with useless referrals and leads.

And that last snitch—he was certainly an ill-fitting link. The Texan had come totally out of left field. Preston felt sure the man had a hidden agenda. He fully intended investigating the company the Texan had mentioned, but had turned down the man's offer to accompany him there.

An offer like that he could easily refuse.

At the moment, his problem was finding Ford, who had done a disappearing act on him.

Preston had considered accompanying Clementine back to the resort, hoping he could get some real an-swers instead of evasive ones. But she had assured him she'd be all right, and, concerned about Ford, who had blithely dismissed the possibility of danger, Pres-ton had returned to the restaurant only to find his un-cle gone.

His thoughts went from Clementine, to the snitch parade, to Ford, and back to Clementine. The lady had him stumped.

She had seemed attractive, capable, delightful.

She had *not* seemed to be the stuff of which crimi-nals were made.

But in his many years of experience as investigative reporter and all-purpose snoop, Preston had met many a woman who looked, acted and smiled like an angel, and had turned out to be the proverbial devil in disguise.

And that bit with the seduction... Clementine knew he was attracted to her. She could be using that attraction to keep his attention diverted. Preston would certainly like to think Clementine shared his feelings—steamy and X-rated—but he had the distinct impression that Clementine had been acting a part. She had struck him as the honest, up-front type. His kind of woman, for he didn't like to play games, either.

Talk about a rock and a hard place. Preston wanted to believe Clementine was just as drawn to him as he was to her, but if he let himself believe that, and her interest was faked, many people, including his uncle, could be in danger.

Putting his notes away in a hiding place he'd devised in his suite, Preston went in search of his uncle.

Clementine decided to go back into town. Luckily, even though the insect lotion stunk to high heaven, it was colorless. Her skin looked a bit oily, but that could pass for sun block. Putting on a short, yellow halter dress, which had a minimum of contact with her upper body, she quickly left the hotel.

Besides looking for her mother, Clementine wanted to find a weapon. She had not been allowed to bring her registered gun with her, but she was sure that offering a generous sum in certain quarters would procure what she required in no time.

The fair-haired man saw Clementine leave the hotel and motioned to a car waiting in the shade of a *sauce llorón.* The island was awash in weeping willows, and they certainly provided good cover.

The man fastidiously cleaned the seat of the Renault before getting in, making sure his white suit remained impeccably clean.

Five

Clementine felt her frustration mounting. Her mother seemed to have disappeared into thin air!

She had located the couple who had introduced Celeste to scuba diving, but they said they had dropped her off in town and seen her talking to a tall, well-built blond man.

A new urgency was firing up Clementine. In a case like this, she'd rather err on the side of her mother, so she decided that Ford was guilty until proven innocent. If he *were* blameless, well, she could always apologize later.

Apologies were easier given and received than condolences.

At one point in her search, Clementine had caught sight of Preston, and he'd also seemed to be searching for someone. Another selection from that smorgasbord of disreputability?

Although Clementine had no solid proof that Preston and Ford truly *were* nephew and uncle, her instincts told her they were. Besides, they looked too much alike not to be related. And there seemed to be genuine affection between them. They shared an easygoing banter that could only be developed through trust and a long acquaintance.

But the fact that they were most likely related did not leave either off the hook. After all, they could be partners in crime. And until either or both were cleared by Peter, that's what she would consider them.

Luckily, she'd been able to acquire protection, a snub-nosed .38. It wasn't her weapon of choice—too small, and not powerful enough—but it was better than nothing when facing the unexpected.

Now, if she could just find Celeste...

Preston caught sight of Clementine hiding in the shadows of a pet store. Many people visiting Isla Gaucha ended up taking an animal home. Customs regulations were lax, and recently divorced folk often felt the need to fill the void with something else to love. But although his uncle had seriously considered acquiring an animal, Preston doubted that was Clementine's motivation in being at the pet store.

The Radcliffe Research Compound, headquartered on Isla Gaucha, was world-renowned and acquired animals through donations, breeding and even abandonment. It was a veterinary clinic of sorts, and if the animals nursed to health were not endangered, a new home, private or public, would be found for them. There was only so much room at the compound.

There were rumors of smuggling, but direct involvement by the Radcliffe Center had never been proven. Rather, customs officials were widely suspected, since they did not strenuously interrogate anyone about where they came from or what they were doing on the island.

Shaking his head, Preston felt worry squeezing his heart like a vise. Clementine was certainly behaving suspiciously.

Not only had Ford vanished, after having waxed poetic about the opportunity of spending some time with his favorite—and only—nephew, but now Preston had to face the possibility that Clementine might have been involved in his uncle's disappearance.

What had she been doing in the jungle on two separate occasions? Did she have some business she wanted to keep secret? Or had that first time been a ruse to ensure meeting him—and through him, Ford? After all, his uncle was a wealthy financier and his breakup from his wife, his junior by twenty years, had been written up in the social pages. Was Clementine trying to become the new Mrs. Rutherford Kilpatrick, with hopes of sharing in his sports enterprises? If not, why had she asked those strange questions in the lobby, pretending that she didn't know that Ford was from California? Was Clementine really from Denver? Just accompanying her mother while Celeste got her divorce? If so, why had she followed him all over town, and into the restaurant where he had arranged to meet Ford? And what was she doing back in town, when she ought to be in her room, relaxing and recuperating from those nasty scratches and bites?

And there was another, even more chilling possibility: Just because everyone assumed the "Iceman" was a man did not mean the ringleader could not be a woman....

* * *

"Thank you for agreeing to dine with me. My nephew deserted me to escort your daughter to the *farmacia,* and I assume, back to the hotel. I was ready to forgo dinner in town, when I saw you waiting for a taxi."

As Ford held out a chair for Celeste, she smiled, and said, "The pleasure is mine." Looking around the discreet, elegant establishment with an approving glance, she asked, "How did you find such a treasure off the beaten path?"

"Small world, small island," Ford told her. "Besides, I have my sources." As a waiter approached them with gold-embossed menus, he asked, "Are you hungry?"

"Always," Celeste said with an impish smile. "And not only for food."

Ford's dark blond eyebrows formed exaggerated commas over his blue eyes. "Your husband—"

"Soon-to-be-ex," Celeste corrected pleasantly. "I'm still fond of him, but I realize he'll never take my first husband's place." Sipping from a water goblet, Celeste added, "Obviously, if our marriages would have been perfect, neither one of us would be here."

"I can see where Clementine gets her frankness," Ford told her, feeling a blush creeping up his tanned neck.

Celeste laughed delightedly. "And I can see where Preston gets his sensitivity. I never dreamed I'd see a man blush again, let alone two in such a short span of time."

"Oh?" Ford said leadingly.

"Your nephew shares your quaint habit. Clementine apparently embarrassed him, and he was turning redder than a cranberry."

Ford doubted the statement. If anyone would do any embarrassing, it would be Celeste, not Clementine. But he didn't want to ruin the mellow mood over such an inconsequential white lie. It had been a long time since a woman had pursued him for something other than his vast holdings. It felt nice to be wanted, and he had to admit Celeste fascinated him—to say nothing of his attraction to her face and figure, which were in the knockout category.

"You know, I think your daughter and my nephew would make a great couple."

"That's what *I've* been thinking! I've been trying to get the two of them together—first subtly, and then with a sledgehammer. Even Clemmie, who has seen me at my worst, has been surprised at my heavy-handedness. But with Clemmie, there is no other way. She dates occasionally, but her real love is her work."

"Her work?" Ford asked as he caught the eye of the waiter who had been patiently waiting for his signal by the tropical garden that served as an outdoor café.

Celeste and Ford ordered, and Ford asked the waiter for an orchid. When it arrived, Celeste was the one who blushed with pleasure.

"Ah, so the forward lady is not as tough as she makes out," Ford teased, enchanted. Celeste looked like a teenager on prom night, her eyes aquamarine stars. Spying some suspicious wetness in them, Ford asked, alarmed, "I haven't offended you, have I? Gotten the signals crossed? I know neither of us is actually divorced yet..."

"A mere formality," Celeste said dismissing his concern with a wave of her slender, perfectly manicured hand. "It's just that it's been a long time since anyone has given me a corsage, or flowers that did not have birthday or anniversary attached to them. That's one of the reasons I'm divorcing Ronald—he used to be very romantic and attentive, but lately he's been away so often . . . and I am a woman who demands a lot of tender loving care. . . ." Celeste stopped, feeling she had said too much. She normally did not confide in strangers—although Ford was quickly becoming more than that. And she didn't want to burden him with her marital difficulties, especially when he had his own divorce to think about.

Ford breathed easier, and found his heart was becoming more and more ensnared by this lovely woman. She really was unpredictable—and fun, and lovely.

Feeling like a teenager himself, Ford sought to get himself under control. "You were saying about your daughter's work?"

Celeste leaned forward, looking into Ford's dark blue eyes with her luminous aqua ones, and told him, "I swear, at this rate I'll never get any grandchildren. Clemmie is married to her career—a private investigator, no less, something I like to keep from promising male prospects at first."

"You told him *what?*"

Clementine, her nerves shot with worry over Celeste's disappearance, as well as over some of the rumors she'd picked up in town, had to keep from screaming at her mother. The hotel lobby was certainly not the place to conduct an argument, but Celeste was offended and not budging.

"Don't tell me you wanted to keep it a secret?" Hands on her hips, Celeste began to look really annoyed. After all, she'd listened to Clemmie go on and on for ten minutes about some danger, and about how irresponsibly she'd acted for taking off without notifying her daughter first.

"I am *your* mother, remember? I do not have to account to you for my actions."

Clementine breathed deeply, counting to ten. One thing mother and daughter shared, in spades, was a doozy of a temper. Slow to flash point, but a real beauty when the explosion came.

Of course, her mother was a grown woman—and unaware of any danger.

"All right, Mother, I'm sorry if I flew off the handle—"

"I should say so! First you give me periodic lectures as to how the man you fall in love with—if that day ever comes—has to accept you for what you are. And now that I'm breaking your occupation to Preston slowly, via his uncle—"

"I, too, am a grown woman, Mom—"

"A mother's prerogative," Celeste said dismissively. "Besides—"

"And how do we know they really *are* who they say they are, let alone nephew and uncle," Clementine cut in.

Celeste shook her head. "Clemmie, Clemmie, you've been reading too many detective stories..."

"I live them, remember?" Clementine reminded her mother. "Besides, I don't have much time for reading."

"More's the pity," Celeste said. "You don't have enough leisure time. And do you have to look for ulterior motives in everyone? This was supposed to be a restful vacation for you."

"Chalice Investigations has a thriving business because people are far too trusting, and realize too late they've been duped." Clementine knew that despite Celeste's astuteness and intelligence, she was not a cynic. Her mother still liked to think the best of everyone, and gave people a second chance. In her business, Clementine had learned to distrust first, and ask questions later.

Celeste frowned. "I don't like what your profession is doing to you, Clemmie."

"Don't worry, Mom, it has not turned me into a man hater, or into a total cynic." Celeste snorted, and Clementine added contritely, "But you don't know anything, and I blame myself for not filling you in sooner."

"Those wild rumors you just mentioned are just that," Celeste said, unconcerned. "These divorces have been going on for over four years, and they are more popular than ever. As for Ford and Preston being uncle and nephew, I am convinced of it. Just as I know that Ford is a sports entrepreneur *and* perfect gentleman."

"Because he gave you a wild orchid?" The moment the words were out, Clementine wanted to recall them. The hurt expression on her mother's face made Clementine feel as if she were back in grammar school, disappointing Celeste with a bad report card. "What I mean is—"

"What you mean is that I am so desperate for male companionship, and such an easy mark on the re-

bound, that I can't tell when a man is the real thing."
Drawing herself up to her full height, Celeste held her
back stiff and added, "Despite your sad opinion of
me, I am a *very* good judge of character. I intend to go
out with Ford tomorrow, after he gets his divorce, and
I also plan on celebrating with him after *my* divorce.
For now, I'll be in the bar trying to forget your own
lack of judgment and manners."

Clementine watched helplessly as Celeste headed for
the bar, her head so straight it looked as if her neck
would snap. She had really done it...antagonized and
hurt her mother, and now Celeste would not even
consider the possibility that she could be in danger.

How real that danger was Clementine would ascer-
tain soon enough—if Peter had been able to get the
information she'd requested.

Clementine rushed off toward her *casita*, trying
hard not to run and draw any more attention to herself.

Preston looked at the pearl gray business card that
said Clementine Cahill, Chalice Investigations, and
shook his head.

He'd been unable to gather information about
Clementine from her possessions, but *Celeste's* belongings had produced the telltale card.

Apparently, Clementine had made sure nothing
gave her away after her suspicions were aroused, but
obviously Celeste was proud of her daughter and her
potentially dangerous profession.

But if any of his fellow reporters in the investigative branch of the paper got wind of this, he'd never
live it down. A private dick. Clementine Cahill from
Denver, Colorado, a respectable businesswoman...

and he'd thought *she* was involved in the crime rings on Isla Gaucha.

That there *was* something going on, of that there was no longer any doubt. Tony Esperanza was very dependable. Tony and he went a long way back, when they had both started as cub reporters in California. Then Tony had gone back to Florida to marry his college sweetheart, and had stayed there. They talked to each other periodically, and saw each other once or twice a year.

Although Preston had not been able to locate Ford, while in town he'd been told that his uncle had been seen at an elegant restaurant in the company of a petite, beautiful blond lady. Celeste Cahill.

Knowing that he could beat Clementine to the hotel, Preston figured he might get some information about her by searching her room. Not very ethical, but then he had the feeling Clementine would have no compunction in searching *his* belongings if she suspected him.

Preston had also wanted to make sure that his attraction to Clementine did not blind him to the fact that the business card could be a phony, and her business a cover. A couple of discreet inquiries back home had taken care of that, and now he was mooning over the card with a silly smile on his face.

Ford was all right, and Clementine was not a criminal. Life was good!

As he sat on a large, comfortable bed, Clementine's card cradled in his palm, Preston's mind became crowded with thoughts that had nothing to do with crime rings or investigations. Unless they involved investigating the scrumptious body of Clementine Cahill, Private Eye.

Preston was so lost in erotic daydreams that he did not even hear the door open.

But he heard the icy voice that pinned him to the mattress.

"What the hell do you think you are doing on my bed?"

Six

——

Preston looked appreciatively over the hourglass figure in a tiny yellow dress. Hiding Clementine's business card, he answered, "Waiting for you."

Clementine swallowed. Preston's gray eyes were lambent flames palpably caressing every inch of her body. With a start, she remembered having given him the wrong impression—and realized she'd have to keep up the charade a little longer until she could get on the phone with Petey.

Pushing down her fury at his impertinence, Clementine managed to say in a controlled voice, "How did you get in? I don't recall giving you a key."

"An oversight, I'm sure," Preston said, enjoying himself. He had begun to realize that Clementine must have suspected him, just as he had suspected her. It made sense that she would try to protect her mother, just as he'd been trying to protect his uncle. And that accounted for her pretense.

Luckily, he thought, Clementine earned her living as a detective . . . or she'd have lean years ahead of her as an actress.

Clementine probably did not know he was a reporter yet, but she would soon. So . . . no better chance than the present to get to know Ms. Cahill a bit more intimately. Especially since he was fairly sure she was not totally indifferent to him.

He fervently hoped she wasn't.

Patting the bed, Preston suggested, "Why don't you join me? You must be really tired after all that running around."

At his suggestive words and smile, Clementine's blood pressure threatened to hit the ceiling, but she bit her inner cheek. Boy, she was bound to be scarred for life before she was through with Preston!

"I think I'd like a breath of fresh air. Why don't you join me on the veranda?" she said.

Seeing genuine disappointment on Preston's face, Clementine did not wait for a rebuttal. She quickly went to the French windows, opened them and stepped outside into the hot, humid air. Her body begged for the coolness of the huge ceiling fans in the *casita*, but Clementine resisted the demands of her weak flesh. Even if she were forced to melt into a puddle, she was going nowhere near that bed.

Preston's voice, so deep and close, startled her. "This part of the resort is inspired, isn't it?" he said, his breath stirring the hair at her nape and shoulders.

Alarmed at the pleasurable sensation—after all, Preston was a complete rogue and an opportunist, to boot—Clementine quickly sat down . . . and regretted her decision as Preston just as swiftly dropped next to her, preventing any escape from the love-swing.

When speech failed her, Clementine cleared her throat.

God, how she hated the knowing glint in this hateful man's gorgeous gray eyes!

"Well, the rooms are not too luxurious—"

"They aren't supposed to be—just comfortable and relaxing," Preston countered, somehow managing to inch even closer, and making her feel less than relaxed.

"And the *casitas* are very similar to the ones at El Conquistador in Tucson—"

"But you can't match the view," Preston said, his voice dropping another octave as he lowered his gaze to the ruffly neckline that bared the top of her breasts.

Clementine twitched her shoulders. She felt like Little Red Riding Hood with the Big Bad Wolf about to devour her. The combination of potent virility, lingering after-shave mixed with body heat, husky voice and hungry silvered eyes made her ultrasensitized all over.

Hoping for something to distract her, Clementine looked around her. "The mountains and waterfall are nice—"

"But this is nicer," Preston said, putting one hand on her knee, and letting his fingers do the walking in a mind-destroying caress.

Clementine's eyes followed the path of those oh-so-very expert hands as they slowly inched upward, taking the full yellow skirt with them and baring her softly muscled thighs.

"Your muscle tone is splendid," Preston murmured, massaging the firm flesh. Looking into her eyes, he added, "And your shoulders and back are just magnificent."

His other hand looped around a spaghetti strap and pulled so it rested halfway down her arm.

"You have the softest skin," Preston said against her shoulder. His words tickled her heated flesh, and added to the maddening stimulus of his other hand doing sinful things to her thigh, they began a nuclear meltdown inside her lower body that owed nothing to the tropical January heat.

Clementine was barely able to control the moan that emanated from deep within her. Frantically, she grabbed his hand, stopping the upward progress that had gotten dangerously close to a throbbing part of her. Putting Preston's hands in his lap, Clementine noticed that he was certainly not unaffected. The straining bulge against his dark blue slacks was quite visible and provided another erotic charge—one she had to immediately resist or risk succumbing to.

"Preston," she said, and when the word sounded more like an invitation than an order to desist, Clementine repeated his name in a sharper tone, moved away from his lips and set both hands against his broad chest.

Preston raised bedroom-sleepy, sexy gray eyes to her, and said, "Yes, sweetheart?"

The endearment threw Clementine for a moment, during which Preston moved one hand to her waist, and plunged the other into her hair, which fell around her flushed face and down her back in wild waves.

Clementine swallowed audibly, and closed her eyes as one hand traveled over her skin, dispensing magic to her bare back, and the other massaged her scalp, relaxing her into mindless oblivion.

"You are so beautiful, Clemmie. I must thank that gorgeous mother of yours for the great genes."

Preston realized his mistake an instant before Clementine opened her eyes and stiffened in his arms.

Clementine's hands, which had unconsciously begun to travel over his chest, stilled, and she pushed against Preston.

"Mother!"

The alarm in Clementine's voice would have been funny had Preston not been in so much pain near the region of his zipper.

For as Clementine yelled "Mother" in Preston's ear, one of her hands slipped over the silky material of his blue shirt, and inadvertently—but literally—hit Preston below the belt.

Preston's breathing stopped, and Clementine could have sworn the heart underneath her other hand had ceased to beat, too.

For a minute, time seemed suspended. Clementine concentrated her gaze on the light blue material beneath her right hand, and made sure the culpable left hand disappeared behind her.

After an endless moment, Clementine looked up and saw some color returning to Preston's face, white beneath the tan. His usual blinding grin looked out of kilter, and he cautiously moved away from her on the swing.

"All you had to do was say no," Preston told her in ragged gasps.

Clementine's gaze automatically slid downward, but she saw that Preston had one hand protectively covering the area.

"Sorry. But I do have to go and pick up Mother," Clementine lied smoothly. "And I am sorry about the—accident. It really was."

Preston smiled ruefully. "Just as well. A few more minutes, and I would have had another accident, and you'd be getting me a fresh pair of slacks from my room."

Getting up carefully, Preston stood for a moment, taking deep gulps of the humid air.

"I'm sure you can see yourself out, since you had no trouble finding your way in," Clementine told him wryly.

"Your wish is my command," Preston said, trying a bow, but failing to bend all the way down from the waist. "I'll just beat a careful retreat," he told her, his eyes dark gray with the remnants of pain and smoldering desire.

As she watched Preston leave her *casita*, Clementine shook her head. While she was glad to have survived Preston's masterful seduction fairly intact, she reflected that her career as a Mata Hari had just been finished.

She'd better leave seduction scenes to those more qualified and inclined to stage them, because she had almost gotten hoist upon her own petard.

As Preston was making his bowlegged exit from Clementine's *casita*, two men were making their way into the Puerco Loco.

"You take Kilpatrick's room, I'll take the looker's. Just make sure no one sees us—you know what the boss said. If we can't bug them tonight, we'll do it another time."

"I would certainly like to bug that dame personally, you know what I mean, Texas?" the younger man, a redheaded Goliath, told his partner.

"Cool down, boy. And don't use any names! Remember...anonymity. In your language, mental midget, that means do not let anyone know who we are."

Seven

"He's *what?*"

As Peter gave Clementine the dope on Rutherford and Preston Kilpatrick, sports magnate and investigative reporter respectively, Clementine's incredulity changed to fury and then self-disgust.

And to think she had been willing to sacrifice her body—well, not all the way, and come to think of it, it would not have been such a hardship. Clementine whipped up her rage again before she got lost in remembered lust and forgot Preston's duplicity. "And you say he was making inquiries about me?"

That took the cake! Fuming, Clementine conveniently elected to ignore the fact that she had been investigating Preston and Ford, herself.

"You've got a wide network, boss," Peter was telling her. "And that friend of yours, Nelson Madigan in California, called to alert you."

"Why, Preston, you rat fink," Clementine mumbled. She did not know what she was madder about: the fact that Preston had known who she was and had chosen to take advantage of the situation, or the fact that he had found out who *she* was before she had discovered *his* identity.

What a despicable, sneaky, two-faced, loathsome cad...

Peter's voice barely got through Clementine's mental sorting of her library of insults.

"I thought you'd be pleased. That means your mother is not in any real danger—at least not from that quarter."

Clementine started guiltily. She'd been so self-absorbed in anger, embarrassment and one-upmanship that she had almost forgotten that vital point.

"You're right, Petey. Just cancel the reservation for Mom's flight out. She can proceed with her divorce as planned." And I can proceed with *my* plan, Clementine told herself, righteous indignation stiffening her spine and resolve.

She realized Peter was waiting patiently on the other end, and said belatedly, "Great work, Petey. Thanks a lot. I'll call you tomorrow, okay?"

"Okay. And boss?"

"Yes, Petey?"

"Please take care. You don't want to get in too deep."

Peter was nothing if not observant.

"I've trained you well, my boy. But don't worry. I know how to take care of myself."

"And be careful with whatever else might be going

on," Peter reminded her.

"I will, Petey."

After putting some more cream on her bites and scratches, Clementine changed and went downstairs in search of her mother.

Clementine saw Celeste was still in the bar, only she was not alone anymore.

Ford had joined her.

About to go into the upscale restaurant for a solitary dinner, Clementine caught sight of Preston entering the lobby. Hiding quickly behind a marble black-and-gold column, Clementine saw Preston questioning the desk clerk.

It probably had something to do with his uncle, because the clerk pointed in the direction of the bar.

Preston approached the bar, obviously saw Ford with Celeste, and halted in his tracks.

Curious, Clementine stepped from behind the column to get a better look. Would Preston be opposed to his uncle and her mother's hitting it off?

Clementine couldn't tell, because as soon as Preston turned, he saw her, and his expression became guarded.

Changing directions, he strode toward her.

Clementine froze, panicky. Her common sense told her to flee. Her instincts were telling her this man was dangerous to her peace of mind.

Yet the part of her that had been humiliated by a novice wanted satisfaction.

Clementine reached a decision as Preston reached her side.

It was too soon for payback time. Besides, her bites and scratches were still bothering her. While Preston's caresses had been sheer heaven on her sensitive, itchy skin, Clementine dared not initiate another encounter. Her nerve endings were too raw yet, and her fury had not abated. Anger and lust did not make good bedfellows, and she needed a cool head and fit body to extract revenge.

"Seen something you don't like?" Clementine asked Preston with a saccharine smile.

"What do you mean?" he asked, trying to mask his misgivings. Had she found out about him already? He hoped not, because he felt he owed her an explanation.

"My mother and your uncle...you don't approve?"

"It's not my place to approve or disapprove, but as a matter of fact, I think they're ideal for each other, don't you?" Preston asked, his frown clearing. Maybe Clementine was upset because she thought he would try to dissuade Ford from a relationship with Celeste.

"I wouldn't go so far as to say ideal, but yes, I think they might be on to something."

"Like us?"

Clementine felt like wiping that smug grin off his face. Deceitful, unprincipled ruffian...

Instead, she said, "The last time we were together, I don't think I left you with a very good impression of me."

"Oh, I forgive you," Preston told her generously. "But if you think you need further absolution, why don't you make up for it by having dinner with me?"

"I would, but I have to make some phone calls to my office in the States—"

Making a show of looking at his watch, Preston said, "Even with the time difference, it's already late. Why don't you wait until tomorrow?"

Clementine's smile threatened to congeal on her face. The unmitigated gall of the man!

"Well, I don't know. I've had trouble getting through today... it must be all that sub-zero weather and heavy snowstorms that are buffeting the northern part of the States—"

"I'm sure you'll have better luck tomorrow."

"All right. You talked me into it."

Pleased at her easy acquiescence, Preston put his arm around her waist and began to lead her into the dining room.

Clementine smiled cheerfully at him, and said, "I feel like dancing tonight. I hear they have an absolutely divine calypso band, and I just love to cha-cha and rumba. Don't you?"

Preston swallowed with apprehension. "I must confess, dancing is not my strong suit, especially Latin dancing."

Clementine's eyes glittered like aquamarines. "Trust me. You haven't lived until you've done the lambada."

Ignoring Preston's sickly grin, Clementine looped her arm through his and led him to the Boleadoras Ballroom, which was adjacent to one of the bars.

"And while we're at it, why don't we invite your uncle and my mother along? I'm sure they would love to join us for dancing and dining."

The next two hours were excruciating for Preston. He had never known there were so many muscles that could be sprained in the human body, nor so many ways of suffering sensual torture.

Preston felt his hard-on would become a permanent fixture.

If he had not known better, he would have suspected Clementine was paying him back for the episode on the love-swing.

Although, looking back, he had not fared too well at the end of that accident, either.

Starting with a rumba, then a cha-cha, then the conga, then the limbo and finally the lambada, Clementine had forced his resisting and resenting body into a human pretzel. Preston considered himself a jock, but the flexibility exercises he did before running or playing any sport had not prepared him for the rigors of Latin ballroom dancing.

The tango had been sheer agony. It was not that Preston was totally lacking in rhythm, but having been put through the paces by Clementine was worse than a whole year of marine boot camp.

"Isn't this fun?" Clementine asked him, her face flushed, her eyes shining, her hair living flames that sparkled under the brightly lit chandelier.

As Clementine brought her hips in close contact with Preston's, and his aching groin became meshed with hers, he could only wipe at his beaded forehead, and grin through his teeth.

Clementine brushed her upper body against his chest, and reminded him, "You're supposed to twirl me."

Preston clenched sore jaws, and did as she requested. When Clementine landed abruptly in his arms at the end of the figure eight, she laughed with joy.

And Preston groaned with unfulfilled sexual desire.

Discreetly checking out the other males in the room, Preston saw that none of them had visible erections. Of course, they were used to this type of dancing and probably actually enjoyed the satanic activity, he thought ruefully.

Preston's body felt totally abused, from top to bottom. The only exercise he wanted—needed—right now, involved a laughing, sexy redhead who was gossamer light on her feet and who was like a stick of dynamite anywhere near his aroused anatomy.

But preferably with no clothes on, stretched out on a soft, king-size bed.

While mercifully the musicians took a break, he looked down and saw that the shirt he'd had the foresight to untuck from his pants was hiding any indiscreet evidence.

Preston was afraid to face himself in the mirror. He must look a wreck. He had originally entered the ballroom looking respectable in slacks, a shirt and sports jacket. He had discarded the jacket almost immediately at Clementine's request, and he had pulled his shirt out of his pants as soon as he saw what the dancing would entail.

If this is what people down here did for dancing, what in heaven's name did they do for sex?

No wonder they looked so happy all the time.

Clementine had never been a tease, but she was disappointed in him. Somehow, she had thought he would possess stronger moral fiber. She had waited for him to apologize for being in her room and to tell her he knew she was a private investigator, but he had yet to do so.

As a slow dance started, Clementine decided to take pity on him and give him another chance.

"You never did tell me what you do for a living, Preston," she asked him, snuggling against him and hiding a smile as she felt him put a couple of inches between them.

"We haven't really had time to discuss anything on this hades of perpetual motion, have we?" Preston said grouchily. Looking at her, he asked half-mockingly, half-seriously, "Do you know where I could find a good chiropractor on this island?"

Her laughter, clear and lyrical, rang through the room, melding with the soft music.

"What's the matter, Kilpatrick? Can't stand the heat?"

Preston's eyes turned almost black. "Shouldn't I be asking you that?"

Clementine's laugh died in her throat at the look of unadulterated passion Preston gave her.

"I'm quite willing to put the fire out—anytime you say," he said.

Clementine gulped. She'd better quit while she was ahead.

Luckily, the band finished the love song, and decided to take a break.

Celeste and Ford came over, and Ford suggested, "Shall we go in to dinner, Clementine? Your mother has put me through the paces—as you've evidently done with poor Preston here—" Preston gave a tired smile in agreement "—and I find I am famished. How about you two?"

"Oh, I'm starving," Preston answered huskily, his eyes hot and dusky gray. "What about you, Clementine?"

"Oh, call her Clemmie," Celeste said.

Clementine used her mother's statement to break Preston's iron grip on her senses. "You know how I feel about that nickname, Mother."

"It's not a nickname, just an abbreviation. Or would you rather Preston called you Tweetie?"

Clementine shuddered. "Clemmie will do."

Everyone laughed at Clementine's pained expression, and they all headed toward the restaurant.

Dinner was a success in more ways than one.

Ford explained that he'd waited for Delores to come in on the evening plane, but his future ex-wife had been delayed because of a storm in Montevideo.

"Hallelujah!" Preston exclaimed.

"Preston!" Ford chided, but Preston grinned unrepentantly. Looking at Celeste, Ford gallantly added, "But I don't mind waiting an extra day to get divorced while I have the company of lovely Celeste."

Celeste regally inclined her head at the compliment, and Clementine suggested, "What about a double divorce?"

"Great idea," Preston seconded.

Ford looked at Celeste questioningly, and when she nodded in smiling agreement, he answered for both, "It's a date. I'll take care of the arrangements tomorrow morning, before my morning jog."

Then, for the umpteenth time, Preston tried to turn the conversation in the direction of careers.

But Celeste forestalled him, and Clementine recognized the pattern. Apparently, her mother remembered their earlier altercation, and, knowing Ford had not had a chance to talk to his nephew yet, was trying to do her daughter's bidding, unwittingly frustrating Preston no end.

From the bemused expression on his face, Ford seemed to have noticed some tension in the air, but apparently had no idea what was causing it.

Clementine had been willing to let Preston off the hook when she saw he was trying to find a way to introduce the topic of their respective professions, and presumably apologize.

But Celeste, once set on a course of action, was formidable.

Which left Ford looking totally puzzled, and Preston royally thwarted. After a couple more forays, and another firm, "Oh, let's not talk shop," from Celeste, he gave up.

The poor man *did* look tired.

Thinking back on the accidental punch to Preston's nether regions, and the sexual tension he'd endured earlier in the day, and then on the dance floor, Clementine was impressed by the man's staying power.

And she was amazed he was still vertical.

Spying Clementine's grin, Preston asked with narrowed eyes, "Would you care to tell us what's so funny, *Clemmie?*"

"Oh, nothing in particular," Clementine answered, laughter threading through her voice. "I just don't remember when I've enjoyed myself so much."

Leaning close, Preston whispered in her ear, "You must have a vicious streak. You always seem to be laughing at my expense."

Startled, Clementine shook her head in vehement denial. "I never did laugh at you during the leeches episode."

"No, only while you were chasing me through the jungle, right? And later on the veranda, and just now in the ballroom from hell?"

Clementine tried containing the chuckles that threatened to erupt at Preston's incensed expression, but it was a losing battle. Throwing her head back, she let loose a cascade of laughter that had heads turning, and people smiling in response.

Celeste and Ford looked from Clementine's laughing face to Preston's glowering one, and Ford asked mildly, "May we share in the joke?"

Clementine looked at Preston, and began laughing again. Preston tried to remain indignant, but her mirth was so contagious that he found himself smiling.

Ford and Celeste looked at each other and said in unison, "Oh, young love," which sent Clementine into further paroxysms of laughter, and even started Preston chuckling.

Preston volunteered to walk Clementine back to her *casita,* but since Celeste and Ford were going to stay at the Boleadoras Ballroom, Clementine politely declined, claiming exhaustion, but staying to watch the dancers.

"You could have fooled me," Preston told her as Celeste and Ford took the dance floor to Gardel's "Mi Buenos Aires Querido." "Dancing before and after dinner—I thought you were unstoppable, and inexhaustible."

"If it weren't for these stupid bites and scratches," Clementine said. Smiling dreamily, she added, "God,

I love tangos. I don't think there is anything sexier on this earth." Looking at the couples intricately twirling and miraculously missing one another on the crowded floor, she told him, "And Carlos Gardel—did you know he was born in France, and grew up in Argentina? My favorite Gardel songs are "Mi Buenos Aires Querido" and "Adiós Pampa Mía..."

"The lyrics are on the tragic side, aren't they?"

"Not all of them," Clementine answered, watching Ford and Celeste gracefully float to the sexy strains. "But yes, some of them are sad, speaking of loss of loved ones, or of missing one's homeland."

Listening to the lovely lyrics, Clementine added, "In this song, the singer talks of the day he once again sees Buenos Aires... 'no habrá mas penas ni olvidos'...there will be no more sorrow or forgetfulness." Seeing that Preston was regarding her thoughtfully, Clementine gave a self-conscious laugh. "Sorry, the songs are melancholic. I didn't mean to get into a soggy mood."

"Oh, don't apologize. I like seeing another side of you." He covered her hand with his big, warm one. "And I like this side, too." As Clementine tried to break contact, he held on. "So you like tangos—you seem to know the words to the songs. Did you take Spanish in school?"

"Grammar school, high school and four years of college, which was hard to do when double-majoring in biology and zoology. With all those required labs, there wasn't a lot of time for electives."

"Zoology?" Preston asked, intrigued. Noticing Clementine's wistful glance at the perfectly matched couple her mother and Ford made on the dance floor, he heard himself ask, "I'll give it another try if you're game."

Clementine looked at him warmly. Preston had really sucked at the tropical beats, but when it came to tangos, he stank supremely. It was really noble of him to volunteer to endure more torment.

"Thank you for your courageous offer, but I've always felt discretion to be the better part of valor." Glancing down at her stocking feet, which Clementine swore showed impressions of Preston's shoes, she added, "After 'La Cumparsita,' I think I have only one functional toe at the moment. And I'd like to keep it for sentimental reasons."

Preston chuckled. "That bad, huh?"

"Worse. You've redefined the meaning of stinking to high heaven when it comes to this type of dancing."

"Jeez, don't hold back." Preston shook his head sorrowfully. "And here I thought I was improving."

"You might one day—but not at the expense of my extremities. Go torture someone at Arthur Murray or some other dance studio—they get hazard pay."

Putting one hand dramatically over his heart and clasping her hand with his other one, Preston said, "You wound me deeply. My confidence will never recover."

Retrieving her hand with a sharp tug that caught him unaware, Clementine said dryly, "Somehow, I doubt it." Putting her shoes back on, she added, "But I'd like to recover full use of my limbs."

As Clementine got up and collected her purse, Preston called out, "Wait, Clem," in an urgent tone, unconsciously abbreviating her name further. No one had ever called her Clem before, and she found she liked it.

But seeing the lights of self-revelation and apology in Preston's silvered eyes, Clementine beat a hasty retreat. She was far too vulnerable right now to deal with apologies and revelations. She had certainly not remained unaffected while putting Preston through such sensual torture.

"See you tomorrow, Preston," she said over her shoulder as she walked rapidly away from the table.

Preston took off after Clementine just as Ford called out to his nephew, "Preston, how about switching partners?"

Preston motioned to his uncle to wait. "I need to talk to you, Clem. Besides, I can help you apply that horse liniment you were prescribed."

Clementine stopped and turned to him. "Thanks for the offer," she declined with a smile, pushing down the exciting images his words evoked. "But I'll manage just fine." Pointing to her mother who was happily waving at both of them, she told him, amused, "I think your services are required elsewhere. I do believe my mother has worn Ford out."

Preston turned toward the couple with a loud groan, and Clementine made a quick, grateful escape.

Eight

After taking a hot bath and slathering the antibiotic cream all over her pleasantly tired body, Clementine found she was not sleepy.

Not being a person who held grudges, Clementine felt Preston had suffered enough for leading her on after audaciously breaking into her *casita*.

Since it seemed they were both attracted to each other, Clementine decided she'd let nature take its course when Preston got amorous again.

Which she predicted would not take too long.

Having Preston stew overnight, knowing he had not cleared his conscience, would certainly reinforce the lesson she'd planned on teaching him.

Which was not to take her lightly. And above all, never to deceive her.

If there was one thing Clementine could not abide, it was a liar.

So she had rented a couple of movies, ordered some hot tea and *alfajores de Mar del Plata*—an Argentinean, pastry-like delicacy—and indulged.

Tomorrow she would work off the calories when she compared notes with Preston, and they investigated the suspicious goings-on—together.

It would sure be fun to cooperate with Preston on and off the job.

In the middle of the second movie Clementine conked out.

The insistent tropical sunlight, along with some heavy pounding lifted Clementine out of a Technicolor dream featuring Preston. Since when did they allow construction crews with jackhammers inside resorts?

Clementine threw back the covers and stumbled toward the source of the irritation with eyes half-closed against the offending morning sun.

The noise seemed to be coming from the vicinity of the door. And it *wasn't* from a jackhammer.

Mumbling nasty things under her breath, and promising dire retribution against whoever had dared intrude upon her sleepy-time paradise so early, Clementine flung open the door without checking through the peephole.

Preston was left with his fist in the air, his body leaning forward to lend more weight to his knocking.

Off balance, Preston fell against Clementine, and held them both up.

Clementine came instantly awake, and decided that maybe reality did have a few advantages over dreams.

Preston seemed to have forgotten the reason he had come to Clementine's room in the first place. His hands began instinctively traveling over her sleep-warmed body, and since all Clementine was wearing was a thin nightshirt that read Private Eyes Keep An Eye On Your Privates, their effect was immediate and explosive.

Clementine found herself lost in Preston's walking fingers. Talk about truth in advertising—the Yellow Pages ads were certainly right!

But it belatedly occurred to Clementine that she shared the *casita* with her mother!

While Clementine shared a lot of confidences with Celeste, she was not inclined to have her mother witness this encounter.

Some things were better left unsaid—and unobserved!

With this in mind, Clementine shoved Preston away, and he moved with alacrity, turning sideways.

Recognizing Preston's defensive posture, Clementine laughed. Would he always shy away from her like a scalded cat? That certainly did not augur well for the relationship she had in mind. She'd better cure Preston of his instinctive, if justified, fear. And fast!

But first things first. She had to get dressed, and out of the *casita* before her mother started making some of her more ribald jokes. No one embarrassed Celeste.

"Why don't I get dressed, Preston, and then you can tell me why you chose to come charging in here like an injured rhino?"

Carefully gauging her mood, and apparently reading it as nonbelligerent, Preston closed the distance between them and embraced her once more, hungrily nipping at her neck.

While Clementine would definitely welcome this menu as a substitute for breakfast any other time, there was still the matter of her mother. When Preston whispered in her ear, "Don't bother dressing on my account," then closed his teeth on her earlobe, Clementine pushed him away.

Enough was enough.

"Preston! My mother!"

The words had a comical and unexpected effect—until Clementine recalled saying "mother" before her unfortunate attack on Preston's private parts.

Retreating once again, Preston pointed toward the empty bed visible in the next room.

"Your mother is not here."

"Of course she's here," Clementine said impatiently, turning to brave her mother's laughing face. "How could she *not* be . . ."

The words died in her throat as Clementine saw that her mother's bed had not been slept in.

Mother?

Before she was divorced?

Shaking her head, Clementine was oblivious to Preston's cautious approach and subsequent butterfly-soft kisses until they reached a mysteriously bared shoulder. Her nipples had noticed, though, and they were poking against the almost-see-through fabric with unbridled enthusiasm.

"Preston, stop!" Clementine demanded without much conviction.

"Time to put up my dukes, get in my martial arts stance, protect the family jewels?" Preston asked wryly even as he backed slowly from Clementine, but kept his arms loosely around her waist. "You know, Clem—" There it was again, his unusual form of endearment... Even Clementine's worry about her mother could not prevent her from smiling fondly at Preston.

"I don't trust that smile," Preston said suspiciously.

Sobering, Clementine pried loose and walked away, putting some breathing room between them. Preston's presence was like the Santa Ana wind, hot, breathtaking, destroying all resistance in its path.

"You're right. This is no time to smile. I have to find out what happened to Mother."

As Clementine walked to one of the closets and picked out some shorts and a top, Preston sat down on the edge of a love seat. "What are you worrying about? Your mother is okay."

Clementine froze, hoping he knew where Celeste was. "Then you saw her downstairs? When I finally dropped off last night, I was dead to the world. I wouldn't have heard a freight train, let alone Mother, who's got to be one of the quietest, most graceful people on earth."

"No, I didn't see her, but I am glad you're showing some aftereffects from all that dancing last night," Preston said, smiling with satisfaction. Rubbing a sore shoulder, he added, "That's some consolation, since I can't seem to get all my working parts to function in harmony today."

"You didn't seem to have much trouble a few minutes ago," Clementine reminded him, holding her clothes against her. Preston's eyes looked like the eyes of a man who had been fasting for forty days. Bending to retrieve some sneakers and socks, she demanded, "Why did you barge in here, anyway?"

"Because *I* was worried about Ford. His bed has not been slept in, either. And he never did make those arrangements for a double divorce."

"Maybe he forgot," Clementine began. Then, when the full import of his words sank in, she asked, "Are you casting aspersions on my mother?"

Preston looked at Clementine blankly for a moment.

"Aspersions?" Then, realizing what she was referring to, he said incredulously, "Oh, come off it, Clem. They *are* two consenting adults—"

"And you just assumed my mother would jump into bed with the first attractive man she met on the island?" Obviously, Preston did not know the urgency of the situation. She'd never told him about the conversation she'd overheard—and now the specter of his uncle's possible involvement in shady goings-on was raising its ugly head again. Ford was thoroughly charming, but who knew what lurked beneath the pleasant facade?

Preston looked uncomfortable. "Of course not, but my uncle and your mother were so *simpático*—they were still dancing cheek to cheek when I left, they must have closed up the place...."

"They might have closed up the place, but my mother would never sleep with a man before divorcing her current spouse first—even if the man is undeserving of her. And for your information, there have been only two husbands in her life—and neither of them—including my father whom I love dearly—are nearly good enough for her."

Preston passed a weary hand over his face. Would it always be like this with Clementine? Blowing hot one minute, cold the next? He didn't know if he could take this seesaw battle. He had always admired intelligent, independent women, but Clementine seemed to have this down to an art—and to a degree no mortal man could hope to match.

Seeing Preston's aggravation clearly reflected on his face, Clementine misinterpreted it.

"Get out! No one—especially *an investigative reporter* who obviously has no sense of ethics—will ever insult my mother with impunity."

Startled by her revelation, Preston recovered quickly.

"I meant to tell you about my job last night, but you didn't give me a chance."

Clementine clutched clothes, undies and sneakers against her chest with one hand, and pointed to the door with the other. "A bit late to apologize." Clementine's chin lifted stubbornly in unconscious imitation of Celeste. She added icily, "You should have come clean before that regrettable scene on the veranda."

"Oh, come on, Clem, don't tell me you weren't enjoying yourself. And just because your scheme to seduce me didn't go exactly as planned—"

"You were on the losing end of that, let me remind you."

"How could I forget? Just don't take things out on me," Preston retorted, becoming angry himself.

"Like mother, like daughter, is that what you're saying?" Clementine asked, her eyes glittering menacingly.

"No, you're twisting everything I say," Preston said between clenched teeth, realizing he was handling this badly. Now Clementine seemed to think he was labeling mother and daughter as easy, and that was the farthest thing from his mind. When played safely, Preston considered sex good clean fun—except when it developed into a special language between two people, as it had between the two of them, and was on the way to becoming between his uncle and Celeste.

But he was having a hard time getting through to Clementine. He had botched things up, and all of Clementine's energy was now expended on worrying about her mother.

"I'm getting dressed, and then I'm looking for my mother." Clementine's earlier doubts about Ford came flooding back. How could she have let down her guard, just because Peter had confirmed Ford's and Preston's identities? How could she have been so gullible, so taken in by Ford's easy charm?

Even if the nephew were legitimate, it did not follow that the uncle had to be. After all, the only thing Clementine could be certain about was that Ford had made a fortune on sports equipment, apparel and nutrition. But fortunes are just as easily lost as made, especially if one had some special problem or vice, like gambling or drugs. Or was the victim of bad financial advice or embezzlement by trusted associates. "And if your uncle has done anything to her, I swear—"

"Oh, for heaven's sake!" Preston said impatiently. "Don't get hysterical on me. Get some coffee into your system so you can think coherently." He walked toward the door. "I'll find Ford and then I'll expect an apology from you."

As Preston slammed out of the *casita*, Clementine stalked to the bathroom and slammed the door shut behind her.

What an infuriating oaf! He'd see who would have to eat crow!

Nine

Arching his back and wiping away the sweat stinging his eyes, Ford decided that jogging in a steamy jungle was bad enough, but having to break trail was even worse.

The confines of the rain forest brush, previously so entrancing, were now perilously thick with fronds, vines and thorns that seemed to reach, tentacle-like, for every inch of his exposed flesh.

He was glad that he had listened to Preston and carried a heavy knife with which to clear a path. What had been intended as his morning run had become something more than he'd bargained for when he'd inadvertently blundered onto this unmarked part of the island.

Ford paused in his arduous hacking. Was that voices he heard up ahead? Or was it only wishful thinking? He couldn't tell how long he'd been gone from the resort, or whether he'd been going in circles. Looking up at the sky was not much use, for the thick fingers of vegetation were perversely closed, not allowing a good look at the sun.

Preston was bound to miss him soon, if he hadn't already, and would come after him.

The problem was, how would Preston find him? His nephew had a nose for news and corruption, but he would never imagine that his uncle had been so besotted that he had forgotten to look where he was running.

Ford shook his head. He must really be tired if he was trying to blame Celeste for his getting lost. It wasn't her fault that he had carelessly wandered off the main trail onto God knew what.

Well, he might as well investigate the noise. As Ford half walked, half tripped forward, he thought he detected some refreshing air. A hallucination?

No, he was not mistaken. The temperature had lowered perceptibly, and sea breezes were providing him with newfound strength.

Lifting his feet out of the soft, dank earth with renewed energy, Ford emerged from the tree line and stumbled onto a golden crescent of sand.

And onto an unpleasant discovery...

After a search for Celeste proved fruitless, Clementine decided to forget for the moment who might be right or wrong, and who owed whom what apology. She called Preston's room and asked him to meet her in the lobby.

In black slacks and a gray shirt, Preston would have been a sight for sore eyes had Clementine not been so scared about her mother.

"Hey, what happened to the woman of steel?" Preston teased as he read genuine fear in Clementine's normally fearless gaze. "Lost your cape?"

When Clementine bit her lower lip, Preston realized she was barely holding together. He put an arm around her shoulders and quickly led her to a couch.

"Come on, don't fall apart on me now. I'm sure nothing's happened to them. They're probably doing what comes naturally."

As a storm cloud gathered in Clementine's blue eyes, Preston held up a hand. "Don't slug me."

Realizing Preston had purposely drawn a response from her, Clementine took a deep breath and gave him a quivery smile. "It's one thing to be in danger myself. It's another to fear for a loved one, and feel so helpless."

Preston nodded. "Except we don't know they *are* in danger." Actually, Preston had begun to worry, too, hoping Celeste had not been caught up in the blackmail ring along with his uncle. Although no one had ever filed a formal complaint, the rumors that the happy divorces made some people less than happy had begun to surface regularly. Apart from the fact that he liked Celeste and hoped nothing had happened to her, Preston knew that if her mother was harmed, Clementine would never forgive him.

And he would never forgive himself.

"Actually, I have something to tell you—"

"You don't know what I overheard—"

They both began and stopped simultaneously, doing the "You first, no you," routine until Preston held up a hand. "Ladies first."

Clementine quickly filled him in on the conversation she'd happened upon in the jungle that first morning after breakfast.

"And you didn't tell me?" Preston asked thunderously. Remembering her weird behavior at the resort and then in town, he added, "So that's why you were as skittish as a cat on a hot griddle."

"Thanks for the flattering comparison," Clementine said dryly. "And you may well recall, we weren't exactly bosom buddies at first."

"Not for lack of trying," Preston reminded her. At her reproving look, he said, "I guess we were too busy trying to outdo each other."

He then told her about his own suspicions involving a blackmail ring on Isla Gaucha, and waited for the explosion.

It wasn't long in coming.

"And you withheld that information from me? How could you? I'm a private investigator, trained in criminology—"

Preston held up a hand again, and gave her the peace signal. "A fact your mother took great pains in keeping from me. Come to think of it," he added wryly, "you didn't exactly scream out your occupation from the rooftops."

Clementine flushed guiltily. "Yes, well, I guess we were too busy mistrusting each other at first to exchange confidential information." And then she added darkly, "But some of us knew earlier than others."

"Some of us are better at investigating than others," Preston said, grinning with infuriating smugness.

The conceit of the man! Regarding Preston through slitted eyes, Clementine decided he still needed to be taken down a peg or two. And she was the woman to do it.

But even though that superior smile of his grated on her nerves, all that would have to wait until Celeste was found, safe and sound. And Ford, too, if he was not involved in Celeste's disappearance.

Preston found his earlier misgivings were a tad unfounded. Yes, it was not easy dealing with Clementine Cahill, but her competitive spirit, her fire, her indomitable drive really did get his juices going.

But other things took priority right now. He had to find Ford and Celeste. And with Clementine's help, they'd be able to double up on ideas and checking out leads. There definitely was an up side to dealing with such a competent woman.

"Why don't we meet in my room to compare notes?" Preston asked, managing to inject the appropriate note of innocence in his loaded question.

"I have a better idea. Let's do it over lunch. I'm not very hungry, but we have a long day ahead of us. We'll work better with some fuel for the furnace."

Realizing she was repeating one of Celeste's dearest axioms, Clementine fairly catapulted from the couch.

Ignoring Preston's challenging look that told her he knew eating was not the only reason she was avoiding his room, Clementine turned on her heel and went to her *casita* to get her notebook.

The blond, handsome man listening to Clementine and Preston's conversation from a camouflaged high-tech surveillance van marked Radcliffe Research Compound shook his head, a soulful look in his eyes.

His gaze stared unseeingly at the colorful sign that read Puerco Loco Veraneante.

"What a pity Clemmie Cahill had to insist on getting involved in my affairs. She was supposed to be here on vacation, but she can't resist puzzles or diving right into areas that don't concern her." Admiration mixed with frustration tinged the blond man's voice. "She's a champion for justice and the American way of life—and a royal pain in the butt. Too bad she couldn't keep her nose out of trouble this time—such a pretty nose, too."

"They don't know anything yet, Iceman," Texas said. "They're running around half-cocked in all directions. I'm not even sure why you wanted them bugged."

"*Yet* is the operative word, my friend," the Iceman said. "It was careless of me to have met you so close to the hotel that day. I didn't think anyone would venture out onto that unmarked trail—but I hadn't counted on Clemmie." Smacking his fist into his palm, the man said with an angry edge to his cultured tone, "I don't want to be caught unawares again. I know Clementine's abilities. She's smart as a whip, and Kilpatrick is no slouch, either."

"But they might notice the plants—"

The blond man shook his head. "They only have suspicions so far—hearsay, rumors, overheard snatches of conversation—as well as the wrong information, which I had the foresight to have *you* and others feed Kilpatrick." The younger man nodded, afraid to voice another misgiving. His voice like velvet-covered steel, the Iceman added, "By the time they collect any hard evidence, we'll be long gone."

The Texan ventured, "Too bad we have to pull up stakes so soon. This was a good gig—"

The Iceman's eyes turned arctic. "Do you have other ideas?" he challenged. The other man shook his head, swallowing painfully. "We can still clean up before we leave—provided no one makes any more mistakes."

The younger man nodded nervously.

Knocking on the side of the van to attract the attention of the driver, the Iceman ordered, "Take me to the beach. I want to personally supervise that transaction."

Turning a polar gaze on the Texan, he added, "And make sure two men stick with Cahill and Kilpatrick at all times—if they split up, your thugs do, too."

Clementine picked up the tail a few minutes after arriving in town. She took the north end, and Preston the south end of town, with which he was already quite familiar.

She checked the zippered compartment of her large purse, feeling the cool metal for reassurance. She was glad she'd had the foresight to purchase a gun.

No one had seen or heard of Celeste or Ford since the day before.

Preston noticed he was being followed as he was leaving the first cantina he visited.

Something did not seem right.

After frequenting several bars and eating establishments, his feeling of dread increased.

Some of the information he was being fed was contradictory, some totally farfetched. It didn't even jibe with what he had already paid for.

After leaving an English pub where a lively argument between British and Irish patrons had ensued, Preston listened to his gut some more.

Why would someone be feeding him the wrong information? He was not a private investigator, did not have any credentials on him, had declared to Isla Gaucha customs that he was on the island strictly for pleasure.

Why would someone be tailing him? As far as everyone was concerned, he was a harmless tourist.

The only common denominator was Clementine.

Which meant that Ford could already be a casualty. It wasn't like his uncle to go running for so long, nor to disappear and break his word about making arrangements for a double divorce.

He had to get to Clem, fast!

Ford halted as four men turned, two of them training automatic weapons on him.

The other two were busy loading a boat with several cages.

Contraband animals!

Ford quickly studied his surroundings, which at first sight were quite pleasant. A natural formation of boulders stretched beyond the surf line, creating a small lagoon. A makeshift dock protruded from the ocean, with another boat tied up to it.

He certainly could not swim for it, nor use the boat for escape, because he'd be cut down before he went a few yards.

But perhaps he could dive back into the jungle, and try to lose himself in the heavy vegetation....

Without allowing himself second thoughts, Ford

turned and ran for cover of the tree line.

He never made it.

En route to the drop-off point, the blond man received two doses of bad news: an intruder had stumbled onto the operation on the beach, and both Preston and Clementine had given their shadows the slip.

Rolling that day's *Wall Street Journal* into an impossibly narrow cylinder, the Iceman gripped the paper until his knuckles turned white.

"I guess I should have expected it. Cahill and Kilpatrick are good, and your goons—" he turned winter eyes on Texas "—are not."

Throwing the newspaper at the younger man with such force it would have taken one of the man's eyes out if he had not ducked, the Iceman said, "We'll have to mobilize. We must leave sooner than planned."

Clementine and Preston met in a prearranged location: the pharmacy where Clementine had purchased the super-smelly liniment.

"How could they have gotten onto us so fast?" Clementine asked, worrying her lower lip. "You don't think—" She looked at Preston, her eyes widening.

He nodded grimly. "Who knows how long they've been listening." Seeing Clementine's look of dismay as she recalled what had transpired between them at the *casita,* Preston playfully tapped her nose, "It's a good thing that you put me out of commission, isn't it?"

Clementine gave him a grim smile. "If someone has harmed a hair on my mother's head, I'll gladly put *them* out of commission."

"Bloodthirsty wench!" he said. Clementine smiled. Preston knew how to beat back the darkness. "Did you do a sweep of your place when you checked in?"

Clementine shook her head. "No, I never dreamed—"

"Don't worry about it. I came here with suspicions, intent on checking a lead and keeping my uncle out of trouble—and I didn't examine my room for bugs, either." Putting his arm bracingly around Clementine's shoulders, he said, "Let's go back and do a cleanup."

They returned to the resort in the same taxi. Since someone was onto them, it was not necessary that they enter the Puerco Loco stealthily.

As they were crossing the main lobby toward the front desk, a voice stopped them in their tracks.

Ten

"Clemmie, Preston, wait up!"

Clementine turned, her heart in her mouth.

After grabbing on to Preston's arm for an instant of intense relief, Clementine flew to her mother's side and embraced her in a bone-crushing hug.

Celeste returned the embrace, a pleased but puzzled expression on her face.

"It's not that I don't enjoy this unusual display of affection—you've always been a bit too much on the dry side, like your father—but I didn't realize my presence was this sorely missed."

When Celeste noticed the tears in Clementine's eyes as she straightened, she joked, "I know I'm the life of the party, Tweetie, but surely you and this gorgeous hunk could have thought of something to do to occupy your time?" Patting her daughter's wet cheek, Celeste said, "Unless you've been in Preston's room, playing hide-and-seek? Because I have not been able to find either of you for the last several hours—''

"Mother!" Clementine interrupted in a voice so abraded, her throat felt as if a knife were slashing it. "How could you?"

"What, look for you? I didn't mean to interrupt anything...you know I'm all for you getting involved, especially with this charming young man...." Celeste's voice trailed off, and she let her hand drop at her side as she read blinding fury in Clementine's eyes.

"What have I done now?" Celeste asked, totally perplexed.

"This is rich...*you* were looking for us!" At first weak with relief, Clementine now felt full strength return to her limbs. She fairly vibrated with anger. "Where the hell were you last night...and this morning?" Fully revved up, she bit out the words. "How could you leave without explaining?"

Celeste's backbone underwent its familiar stiffening. "Young lady, I don't think I owe you any explanations. If anyone will be doing any explaining, it's you, with your Dr. Jekyll, Mr. Hyde imitation."

Foreseeing a tremendous battle between the evenly matched combatants, Preston smoothly intervened.

"Do you think we could move this conversation to a more secluded place? We are attracting a lot of attention."

Both mother and daughter quickly looked around, chagrined at the many avid faces openly watching the confrontation, and making no effort to hide their curiosity.

"Thank you, Preston," Clementine said quietly. "No need to make a scene."

"For once we agree on something," Celeste said huffily, patting her coiffure in a nervous gesture.

After inquiring about Ford once more at the front desk, Preston led the way to his room.

Once in Preston's room, both he and Clementine began doing a cooperative sweep. Celeste, having been given a quick warning, carried on a normal conversation as she observed the proceedings with interest.

"Why were you so upset with me, Tweetie?"

"You know I would never dream of prying, Mother," Clementine said even as she pumped her fist in victory. She had found the first listening device by the window in a huge *gomero,* a South American rubber plant with a beautiful emerald hue.

"Yes, you would," Celeste said.

"Mother!" Clementine said, annoyance raising her voice.

Celeste was startled when Preston jumped several feet in the air and hit his head on a hanging planter that supported several *claveles del aire,* delicate, small, pink and white flowers.

"F-fudgy whiskers!" Preston bellowed, amending his swearword of choice in the nick of time.

When Clementine burst into gales of laughter, Celeste scolded her, "Clementine, how can you be so insensitive? The man is in pain!"

This brought chuckles from Preston, who said under his breath, "In more ways than one."

Celeste threw up her hands in a gesture of mock frustration, and said, "I give up."

Motioning for silence, Preston held up a device he found on the phone.

Clementine countered with one she located on a lamp, and they both headed for the bathroom.

Preston motioned for Celeste to continue talking, and she said, "I'm sorry you were worried, Clemmie. But you know this island is quite safe."

Both Clementine and Preston stuck their heads out at this statement, Clementine rolling her eyes, and Preston shaking an admonishing finger. Celeste gave them an angelic smile, silently signaling she was aware her comment was misleading.

Clementine and Preston resumed their search, and Celeste continued, "But I can see why you would worry, since you didn't hear from me since last night. No doubt you thought I had drowned scuba diving, or crashed when skydiving."

"Skydiving?" Her expression horrified, Clementine's head popped out of the bathroom again, until Preston pulled her back in.

"I told you I was going to have fun, Clemmie. The past year has not been a bed of roses for Ronald and me. You know I married him because he was so different from your father, and seemed to have all the time in the world—and the inclination—to pay attention to me. But lately he's been as occupied as Sterling was, going on business trips all the time."

Clementine knew things had not been going too well with Ronald after the first year and a half, but she was surprised to hear work was the cause. She would have thought dilettante Ronald would become involved with women, not business.

"Why didn't you travel with him?"

"Because Ronald said it would be boring, and that he would be too busy to devote much time to me. As a matter of fact, he was even dead set against my coming here for the 'happy divorce.' "

"I don't blame Ronald for not wanting a divorce," Clementine said.

"Considering how often he's been gone lately, I was somewhat surprised at how adamantly opposed he was. He told me he loves me as much as ever. And he especially disliked getting a divorce in Isla Gaucha. But finally, he had to agree when I told him I was coming here, whether he liked it or not."

Clementine's intention to ask what objections Ronald had to divorcing in Isla Gaucha slipped from her mind as both she and Preston found the curiously shaped bug at the same time.

They both yelled "Got it" simultaneously, and emerged from the bathroom wrestling for the tiny device.

"Having fun, children?" Celeste asked, and Preston let Clementine have the bug, smiling sheepishly.

After collecting all four devices, Preston placed them outside, and closed the sliding glass door. To be on the safe side, he put on the radio to some static between stations, and began to make coffee in the cheery kitchenette. "Clementine was going out of her mind with worry," he told Celeste.

"I guess I didn't even think when I took off in that sailboat," Celeste began in a contrite manner.

"Sailboat?" Clementine asked, totally at sea. "I thought you said you went skydiving."

"That was later this morning," Celeste said, ignoring Clementine's imploring look to the heavens. "I just didn't feel like going to bed when Ford did—"

At Clementine's raised eyebrows, Celeste said primly, "Well, not before I'm officially divorced,

Tweetie. You know I am serially monogamous, as the talk shows like to label us." Celeste looked mystified at the look of triumph Clementine threw Preston. The answering shrug of wide shoulders further baffled her. "Ford didn't feel like staying up all night, because he said he was going to make arrangements so we could divorce together, and he never misses his morning jog—"

"So he *was* planning on running this morning," Preston said, aiming a triumphant look of his own at Clementine.

"Ford said he never skips a day, rain or shine," Celeste concurred.

"And you didn't hear from Ford again?" Preston questioned.

Unaware of the undercurrent of worry in Preston's voice, Celeste said, "No, we didn't spend the night together. I heard some kids planning to go out on an all-night sail—"

"And you just couldn't resist," Clementine finished. This was the impulsive, squeeze-everything-out-of-life mother she knew and loved. "But you could have come back and told me—"

"I did, Tweetie. But you were unconscious, so I figured I'd let you rest. I *did* leave you a note."

"You left me a note?" Clementine asked, surprised.

Celeste nodded. "It's on the table by the French windows leading to the veranda." Seeing Preston smile wolfishly, and Clementine's cheeks turn ruby red, Celeste demanded, "Will you two tell me what is going on? Your body language and meaningful looks are driving me crazy."

"Oh, it's nothing earthshaking," Clementine said airily. "It's just that Preston owes me a bunch of apologies, and I'm thinking of ways to make him pay up."

"I'm willing to take my punishment like a man," Preston said suggestively.

"I'm still here," Celeste said, waving her hands in the air wildly.

As Preston and Clementine looked at her, their gazes blank, Celeste said, "Could we leave the mating courtship for later, and would someone inform me why Preston's room is bugged?"

"Not just Preston's room, Mother," Clementine said grimly. "We're going to have to do a sweep of our *casita* later."

"What?" Celeste jumped from her seat on the couch.

"There's a crime ring on this island—"

"And Preston's recently informed me that someone called the Iceman seems to be the silent partner who operates from the States," Clementine said.

Eleven

While Celeste was informed of everything that had transpired so far, Clementine grew thoughtful.

Preston noticed her expression, paused in midsentence and waited.

"Do you suppose—" Clementine tapped a complimentary pen etched with a gaucho motif against her chin. "Do you suppose the silent partner you mentioned might be this Delores your uncle is divorcing?"

Preston's face clouded. "Are you back to suspecting my uncle? Besides, Delores did not have a mysterious reason for not arriving in time—just a run-of-the-mill storm, although probably not as strong as the one you were dancing up in the ballroom."

"That could have been a ruse—maybe she decided she could use the cover of bad weather to organize some other...activities."

"You're reaching. Delores isn't capable of masterminding an operation of this magnitude."

"Why not? Because she's a woman?"

"No," Preston said flatly. "I suspected you of being involved—but then you're a lot smarter than she is."

Clementine frowned. While she liked the fact—she thought—that Preston thought her capable and smart enough to be a ringleader, she was not flattered that he had considered her a criminal candidate.

"You've said yourself that Delores is brainier than she lets on. And she was certainly smart enough to land your uncle, who, like his nephew, does not strike me as lacking in the intelligence department."

Preston's countenance grew stormy. "Delores is a gold digger, and she plays the dumb blonde to perfection, but Ford saw through that. He was temporarily blinded by her youth and sex appeal... and I guess she does possess a certain charm. You'd be hard-pressed to find someone who dislikes Delores more than I do, but I still say she is *not* clever enough to engineer anything grand scale. Delores is more small-time, an operator who succeeds on the one-on-one."

When Clementine appeared ready to debate his statement, Preston said heatedly, "My uncle is innocent. It's going to be tough enough to find the real culprit, without our being at cross-purposes."

Celeste, who had remained quiet during their lively exchange, suggested mildly, "And why do you two have to be the heroes? Shouldn't the apprehending of these criminals be the job of the local police?"

"The local police look the other way when it comes to smuggling some animals out of the island. A contact that a friend of mine put me onto said the Iceman has several layers of opportunity going on at once—smuggling and extortion. We have no proof the police are actively involved, but we also don't know how far this silent partner's reach is. I was already fed some dummy information—which means this guy is onto me—so for all we know, he could have some cops on the payroll. How do we know which ones? And we certainly cannot go to the American Embassy. By the time they looked into things, it might be too late to do anything for Ford.''

Preston looked challengingly at Clementine, daring her to deny that his uncle was in danger. She didn't rise to the bait, knowing that Preston was genuinely concerned for Ford's safety. Now that Celeste was safely back in the fold, Clementine could be generous and suspend disbelief.

''And we can't afford to allow the trading of rare or endangered species—''

''I knew your studying to be a vet was not a good idea,'' Celeste told Clementine, who disregarded her mother's comment, and added, ''Nor the rumored extortions to go unchecked.''

''In that, Clem and I are in complete agreement,'' Preston said.

''I even overheard one of the lowlifes brag that no one suspects anything, that there is nothing to worry about,'' she said.

''Until you two showed up,'' Celeste said, leaning forward to place her empty mug on the white-and-gray marble coffee table. ''But isn't it obvious these hoodlums are onto you now? You should be staying away, not placing yourselves in further jeopardy.''

Clementine had trouble meeting her mother's probing gaze. What could she tell her? Yes, it's dangerous, please don't worry? Too late for that now, when Celeste had seen her daughter's state of panic over her own temporary disappearance.

"Don't worry, Celeste," Preston said into the charged atmosphere. "I'll make sure Clementine doesn't engage in any foolish heroics."

"Why, you sexist, domineering—" Clementine stopped midsentence when she saw the smile on Preston's face. He really enjoyed baiting her, but his statement had also been made to distract Celeste.

Unfortunately, her mother's attention would not be diverted. "Do you really think Ford is in danger? That he might have been kidnapped?"

"It's the only logical assumption, I'm afraid," Preston said. "He should have been back hours ago, and he would never forget something so vital as making arrangements for the double divorce."

"Do you think he might have gone to pick up Delores, and forgot to mention it?"

Preston took a deep breath. "No, he didn't go to pick up Delores. I've already checked." Shaking his head, he asked Clementine, "You still believe my uncle is involved somehow?"

"Well, he was dressed in white—"

"So are other people on the island."

"He disappeared at opportune times—"

"With all due respect, so did Celeste."

Clementine frowned at even the slightest hint that Celeste would be involved in any criminal activity. Suddenly, she realized that Preston had purposely made the comparison to make her aware of how much it hurt to hear someone accuse a loved one. Forging ahead, anyway, she told him, "The man I saw was also tall, muscular and blond . . . like your uncle."

Preston scowled, but Celeste came to the rescue. "So is Ronald."

Clementine snorted, the idea of elegant, foppish Ronald trudging through the jungle ludicrous. Celeste giggled in response, obviously sharing Clementine's mental picture.

"And Ford was in the vicinity of—"

"What about motive," Preston barked.

Softly, hating to hurt Preston, Clementine said, "Not all businesses stay successful. Especially in today's economy. Maybe he's having a downturn, or he wants more money—wealth is addictive—or he got involved in drugs or gambling—"

"Why don't you just nickname him Al, for Capone?" he said icily. "Hey, let's not forget tax evasion. Oh, and he drowns kittens in the bathtub for entertainment, and runs over old ladies crossing the street in his spare time—"

"All right, all right," Celeste said sharply.

Startled, Preston and Clementine looked at Celeste. Shamefaced, they regarded each other like guilty schoolchildren.

"I don't think dissension between the two of you is going to help anything."

Turning to Clementine, Celeste added, "The bad guys are out there, not in here, Clemmie. You have a right to your point of view, but do you think Preston and you could find a middle ground? Not only is time awasting, but if Preston's hunch proves correct, Ford *could* be in danger."

"You're right, Mother," Clementine said briskly. "Shall we agree to disagree for now, Preston?"

Preston did not look happy, but said, "I expect a full retraction from you later—but as Celeste so eloquently put it, for now, let's just concentrate on the real threat."

They quickly laid out a plan, and instructed Celeste to stay in the *casita*. "Keep all doors locked, Celeste, and don't let anyone in. We'll bring you some food, so you won't even have to open the door for room service until we get back."

Clementine picked up her purse and checked to see that her gun was in proper working order.

"How did you get *that* through customs?" Celeste asked, wide-eyed. She disliked weapons, and Clementine normally kept hers out of sight.

"The same way, I imagine, I got mine," Preston said, walking over to one of the kitchen cabinets and taking out an aluminum-wrapped bundle from the bottom of a *yerba mate* container.

"So that's what that package was," Clementine exclaimed.

"I figured you'd seen me," Preston said, smiling. "I hadn't picked up that you were following me yet, but that's because you're moderately good at tailing people."

"Talking about damning with faint praise," Clementine retorted as she watched Preston walk over to her mother and try to hand her the gun.

That would be the day!

Celeste saw him coming, and said, "Please keep that away from me. I can't stand guns!"

"But I want you to have some protection," Preston protested.

"I wouldn't have the stomach to use it," Celeste told him, getting up and giving him a quick hug and a kiss on the cheek. "But thank you for worrying about me. I have a feeling you'll be needing it far more than I."

Preston returned the kiss, and said, "Don't worry, Celeste. I'll see that your daughter gets back safe and sound."

Clementine rolled her eyes, but for once did not say anything.

Celeste beamed approvingly at Clementine, and told Preston sincerely, "Thank you, Preston. I feel a lot better knowing that you will be her backup."

Preston frowned, obviously not relishing the role assigned to him, but he also refrained from comment. Celeste glowed. Yes, she could just see herself in a maternity and baby store, shopping for Clemmie's clothes and the baby's crib and accessories.

Clementine gave her mother a fierce hug, and Celeste fought back tears. "I realize the best defense is a good offense," Celeste said tremulously, "but I still wish you could call on the local police."

Preston put a bracing arm around Celeste's shoulders, and told her, "As we said earlier, we can't be sure about the locals. And since *someone* is onto us, there's no guarantee we would be allowed to leave the island. It's best to find out what we're up against. That way, we stand a better chance."

He slid the gun into a holster, which he secured in the small of his back, and grabbed a windbreaker from the walk-in closet.

Clementine walked to the door as Preston slipped on his windbreaker. "We'll be right back," she told her mother. "We have to take care of a few things—sweep the *casita* so you can lock yourself in there, as well as get some provisions for our trip and some food for you. Make sure you stay here until we come and get you."

"Be careful, you two," Celeste cautioned Clementine and Preston before they left the room.

Twelve

The two blond, blue-eyed men faced each other.

"I wonder what Celeste sees in you."

Ford's eyes narrowed at the other man's words. Although blood had dried on his forehead, and stung his swollen eyes, he tried to remain erect.

"How do you know Celeste?"

"I, my dear fellow, know her a lot more intimately than you can ever hope to. I just made the mistake of neglecting her, something I intend to rectify this time around."

Ford tried to think through the fog of pain that held his head in a vise. Everything seemed blurry, and it took him a while to make the connection, but he finally did.

"You're Celeste's ex-husband."

"Not yet. And not for long."

Turning to the man who'd been watching over Ford, Ronald Beinor asked, "How much does he know?"

"He hasn't talked. Been out much of the time. But I don't think he knew anything. He seemed just as surprised as us when he stumbled onto the beach."

The Iceman's smile was chilly.

"It doesn't really matter, does it? Whatever he knows, he'll take to his grave."

"What are you going to do to Celeste?"

Ronald's silver-blond head whipped in Ford's direction. "You really got it bad, don't you? Celeste does have that effect on men."

When Ford took a faltering step toward him, Ronald moved forward and hit him in the stomach. Ford doubled over, and dropped to his knees.

"You know, your nephew and Celeste's daughter make a good team—too bad their association will end the same way you will."

Ford's fists clenched, and he tried to stand. "If you so much as touch them—"

"You'll do what?" the Iceman asked. "You know, the irony is deadly. Here I was, ready to retire and enjoy a gentleman's life with Celeste . . . and she decides to divorce me just as I was ready to abandon a life of crime."

With a monumental effort, Ford stood. "You don't deserve someone like Celeste."

"Oh, I think Celeste and I are ideally suited. She doesn't suspect a thing, and won't. To divert suspicion, I'll go through the divorce as planned, and when she is prostrate with grief over the deaths of her daughter and new friends, she'll have good old Ronald to help her get over her pain."

Helplessness and fury washed over Ford, and he launched himself at Ronald.

The Iceman sidestepped easily, and gave him a kidney punch. Ford fell flat on his face, still trying to get up, but a foot on his neck pushed his face into the dirt floor of the hut.

"Don't push your luck, Kilpatrick. Savor the last hours you have left." Shaking his head, Ronald brushed at the dirt on his immaculate slacks. "So far, I've never had to resort to murder—people have been only too happy to be bought off. But I'm left with no choice now, since I know Clementine and your nephew are a different breed. They won't stop until I stop them."

Ford pushed himself up on his elbows, hatred twisting his features.

"Why kill Preston and Clementine? I won't tell anyone anything."

"Oh, I *know* that. But although they haven't yet connected the activities on the island to me, Clementine is much too smart. And I don't know how much that nosy reporter nephew of yours has figured out already—especially since they disabled all the listening devices."

Texas came into the hut, and the Iceman turned to face him. "I told you to send experts, not morons, to do the job. Now we'll be forced to dispose of three bodies."

The swarthy man looked at Ronald uneasily. "Hey, I didn't sign up for anything this heavy. Smuggling and blackmail is one thing, but murder—"

The Iceman's icy gaze pinned him immobile. "Would *you* rather spend the rest of your life in prison? *I'm* not amenable to that." Turning to face

Ford, he added, "I'm used to the good things in life, and without them, life just isn't worth living, is it?"

Ford stared up at him helplessly. "You bastard! If you have any feelings for Celeste, how can you kill her daughter?"

"I *am* rather fond of Clemmie, but the feeling is not mutual. She forced this onto herself with her relentless snooping. She's always disliked me, and it won't take her long to make the connection. If Celeste finds out the truth about my business dealings, I'll lose her. So, you see, I have no other choice but to dispose of Clementine and tie up the other loose ends."

Turning to Texas, he told him, "We're going to have to transfer him. This hut is too exposed."

Texas frowned. "Where to?"

"We'll keep everything centralized. Have two men take him to the research compound. And make sure you tie him up and keep an eye on him. If he escapes..."

"He won't get away," the man guarding Ford promised.

The Iceman looked at the brawny Jamaican, and nodded his head, satisfied.

He fired one last parting shot at Ford.

"Sorry to leave, old fellow, but I have to get ready for a divorce." Adjusting his white coat over broad shoulders, Ronald added, "It's kind of exciting, in a way. A romantic divorce, and an even more romantic second wedding and honeymoon."

Ford tried to get up once again, but the Jamaican kicked him in the head, and Ford slipped back into unconsciousness.

* * *

"How did you happen to learn about this crime ring?" Clementine asked Preston as she shifted her backpack.

They had left word at the front desk that they were going to do some mountain climbing. After setting out in that direction and disposing of the rappeling equipment they'd rented from the hotel, they doubled back and headed for the Radcliffe Research Compound.

"Still too heavy for you?" Preston asked. Although they had removed the heavy climbing equipment and hidden it in a safe spot near the resort, their packs were still cumbersome.

"No, I just need to get used to the weight," Clementine told him.

Preston nodded, and answered her question. "I was doing some investigating on crime cartels in Miami, where Tony Esperanza is based."

"Tony Esperanza?"

"He's an old friend. We go back a long way, and have kept in touch and done favors for each other from time to time. He moved from California to Florida when he married Gloria, who has a large extended family. Tony's parents are dead, he has no other relatives..."

"And you are the closest thing he has to a brother," Clementine hazarded.

"Now that you mention it, yeah, I guess we're family." He carefully sidestepped a dead log obstructing their path. "He told me a source had informed him of some suspicious incidents involving high-level American executives out of an island called

Isla Gaucha. He'd mentioned it once before in passing, about six or seven months ago—"

"But your uncle had not decided to divorce then," Clementine guessed.

"Right," Preston said. "I did tell him that some rumors had been going around about this place, but he ignored them. He said I'm always carrying on about all sorts of rumors, and many of them don't pan out. Which is true."

Clementine reflected that one reason Preston's uncle might not have been concerned was the fact that Ford was the one masterminding the illegal activities. But she kept the thought to herself.

"Why do you think you'll find some answers at the Radcliffe Research Compound? They're very well known and respected throughout the scientific community. As a matter of fact, they're one of the reasons I agreed to come with Mother when she asked me to take a short vacation... my first one in several years."

Preston took a quick look behind him to make sure they were not being followed.

"Your mother mentioned you studied to become a veterinarian."

Clementine grinned. "That was the plan, in high school. Until I worked one summer as a vet's assistant, and realized that actual needles and operations are involved. I don't have the stomach to draw blood, or to cut and sew kittens and puppies up."

"You just like to blow criminals away, right?" Preston teased.

"So far, I've never killed anyone, and I hope I never do. But unlike Mother, I would have no compunction in using the gun in self-defense, and have, several times."

Preston regarded Clementine's sober expression, and nodded his understanding. "I know I'm glad you're on *my* side," he told her, grinning.

Clementine grinned back. "You should be. I'm a black belt."

"But you still got your degrees in zoology and biology?"

"I was undecided as to a career in college. I took some law enforcement courses as a lark, because a friend of mine was intending to join the FBI—"

"Boyfriend, I assume?"

"You assume right," Clementine said, checking behind her to see if anyone was tailing them, although the vegetation was becoming increasingly thick and it was getting more and more difficult to determine if they were being followed. They'd probably have to depend on hearing now, more than sight. "To make a long story short, I did not go into marine biology, and Dwight did not become an agent. He's now a dentist, and I'm a private investigator, although I am active in several conservation organizations, and keep up with reading about ecology and endangered species."

"Which is why you think that the Radcliffe Research Center couldn't be involved."

"It's highly doubtful. Surely they wouldn't jeopardize their lofty standing and substantial grants and donations by being associated with anything shady."

"My source didn't say they were directly involved." Preston shifted his backpack, cursing the humidity. Already his shirt was sticking to his back. "Most likely, one individual there is selling his or her services to the highest bidder. Whenever exotic animals are involved, there are always rich, above-the-law people who don't mind paying top dollar for ivory or animal skin or leather—or even to acquire an almost extinct animal as the latest in status symbols."

Clementine shuddered. "I'm not an animal activist, but I can't understand people who don't respect nature's delicate balance of life, of which humans are only a link."

"And the most dangerous one of all," Preston said harshly. "But it's not only the private collectors who are at fault. Some zoos really don't care where an animal comes from, although that's starting to change."

As the jungle became denser, Preston got out his machete and began hacking at the thick growth. With the humidity making the heat even more miserable, and the insects dive-bombing them, Preston and Clementine found the going extremely tough.

After two hours of chopping and slicing, Clementine volunteered to take over. Shifting her backpack from tender, raw flesh onto another patch of equally abraded skin, she asked Preston for the machete.

"Are you sure?" Preston asked, eyeing Clementine's slender, delicate hands.

Clementine waved her hands in the air, and reassured Preston, "These are tougher than they look."

Reluctantly, Preston handed over the knife.

"Maybe we should have waited until morning," she said, looking up and not being able to see the sky. The jungle, with its impenetrable green canopy, was choking off the last rays of the sun. "It's going to be dark soon."

"That's the idea," Preston said, holding some branches away from Clementine's face as they continued to hack their way through. "I want to make sure we're near the compound by dawn."

As Clementine moved forward, the underbrush thinned suddenly, and she thought she was hearing things.

"Is that what I think it is?" she asked Preston, eagerly slicing through the last of the growth.

The murmuring of a stream reached her, and after a few more hacks, a grassy clearing came into view.

"I guess it's not a mirage, after all," Preston said.

"I think those take place in deserts," Clementine told him as she began running toward the water.

Preston held her back. Cautiously, he moved forward, and examined the glade.

Clementine drew her gun. How could she have been so careless? This was not a forest preserve back home, but the jungle. Danger, both two- and four-legged, abounded.

After a while, Preston waved her in.

"Thank God! We can take off our boots and cool our feet in the water."

As she put her gun away, Preston joined her. He stopped inches from her, and cupped her face in his hands.

Their gazes met, and she saw desire and concern reflected in the silver depths of his eyes.

"Just promise me you'll be careful, will you?" he asked hoarsely. "I couldn't stand to lose you."

The gurgling of the stream, the pungent smell of the earth and the draining heat receded. All that remained was the heady reality of Preston.

Eyes half-closed, she murmured, "I promise."

With a heavy sigh of regret, Preston told her, "Come on. Let's take a short break—we don't have much time."

Three hours later, Clementine and Preston finished setting up camp in a clearing flanked by a roaring waterfall.

As they opened their packs and took out hammocks, they smiled.

"Great minds think alike," Clementine said, vigorously shaking her purple hammock to make sure no unwelcome bugs had moved in.

"Two minds but with a single thought," Preston countered, looking from his black hammock to Clementine's. "I didn't want to seem presumptuous, but we certainly could have saved ourselves some lugging effort."

Clementine shrugged her shoulders. "What doesn't kill you makes you stronger." Walking over to examine Preston's larger hammock, she asked, "Do we really need two of them?"

Preston dropped his hammock on the ground with gratifying promptness.

"I thought you'd never ask," Preston said huskily, his arm curving around her waist.

Clementine's hands curled around his neck, and she closed her eyes as his lips neared hers.

Slowly, slowly, his mouth alighted on hers with the delicacy of a butterfly, and the heat of a wildfire.

She let her hands travel over his back, reveling in the hardness she felt there, in the play of muscles that shifted under her touch.

Against her lips, he murmured, "I've waited for this far too long."

His touch grazed her, almost teasing, and she smiled, whispering, "We've only known each other for a few days."

"But I've waited for you for a lifetime," Preston told her, bringing his hand around to cup her breast.

Her breasts felt suddenly full and heavy, and a deep languor stole over her.

As Preston opened his mouth and stroked her lips with his tongue, circling them, moving maddeningly from corner to corner, she brought her own hands down to his wide chest, trying to secure some sanity and breathing room.

Preston's gaze was wary as it rested on her flushed, upturned face. "Had a change of heart?" he asked with painful resignation.

His willing acceptance of what he viewed as possible rejection filled her heart. He was obviously aroused, but was still willing to let her set the pace.

"No, Preston," she told him, trembling from tenderness and desire. "I'd just like a change in location. Think we could get a hammock up, so the pesky little critters on this island don't get us when—"

"We're butt-naked?" he ended the sentence for her, crushing her against him for a moment, before doing her bidding with amazing alacrity.

"You do have a way with words," Clementine said, laughing, observing his sure movements with pleasure.

She quickly divested herself of her boots, shorts and top, and waited until Preston turned around.

In the firelight, his eyes glowed like antique silver. He began to move toward her, but she asked him, "Mind taking your clothes off, Mr. Kilpatrick?"

He tore at his clothes, his eyes devouring her all the while. Before discarding his shorts, he took out a small packet, and threw it near the hammock.

Clementine approached him slowly, clad only in two delicate scraps of lace.

Her gaze glided over his body, admiring anew the play of sinew, bone and wonderfully bronzed skin, which glowed with health in the illumination from the small fire.

She saw Preston lick his lips with anticipation, and raised her hand to his mouth. He turned his head and kissed her palm, probing the sensitized hollow of her hand with his tongue.

Clementine sucked in her breath, and pulled her hand away to bury it in the soft hair at the back of his neck, and then stroke the sensitive skin behind his ear....

Preston let himself fall back onto the hammock, which began to swing wildly. Clementine laughed, a husky, desire-laced sound which raced through Preston's veins like a brushfire.

Grabbing her wrist, he pulled her forward, and then curved an arm around her thighs.

Giving a gentle tug, he toppled her. Clementine fell forward gracefully, her legs opening and curling around his waist, while he grabbed the trunk of a tree to keep their balance.

Preston grinned at Clementine's joyous laughter, the childish pleasure of her, and pulled down.

Clementine braced her hands on his shoulders and leaned forward slowly, suspended above him, her breasts a tantalizing inch away from his chest.

As their gazes met, she lifted a hand and ran a fingertip from his forehead down to his nose and then his chin. Swiftly, Preston captured her fingertip, ran his tongue around it, and sucked it deeper into his mouth.

Preston's hands lowered to her hips, and he rearranged her so that she was pressing down on his erection. Clementine shuddered, and let herself fall closer to him, the tips of her lace-covered breasts rubbing against his chest.

He lifted his head to her breast, licking the areola through the thin fabric, and slipped his fingers into her panties, beginning to pull them off. She moved her hips to facilitate his movements, and Preston quickly slid the brief scrap of lace down her legs.

As Preston began licking her other breast, Clementine shifted her bottom and her thighs entrapped him. She heard him gasp, and covered his mouth with hers.

Preston's tongue parted her lips and danced in her mouth, tasting, teasing, brushing against hers, invading and withdrawing. His hand slipped between them, and he trailed a line of fire down her stomach, cupping and then caressing, and finally invading her wet warmth.

As his fingers found the tender nub, Clementine felt as if she would shatter into a million pieces. Her moan was swallowed in his mouth, but she pulled away and buried her lips in his neck, biting sharply.

The friction of Preston's fingers increased, and he pushed her away to gain access to her breasts, licking her nipples and then blowing on the distended peaks, until her breath started coming faster and faster, and suddenly she was enveloped in a delicious, warm weakness, a spreading, hot tide of urgency that reduced her world to pure sensation before she spun off into a universe of white-hot, throbbing, quivering pleasure.

Clementine floated down to earth, and rested her forehead against Preston's. "Quite a ride, Mr. Kilpatrick," she whispered, her body still shivering.

"You ain't seen nothing yet," Preston said, putting her hand against his swollen organ. "Would you do the honors, please?"

"With pleasure," Clementine told him, her eyes shimmering as she helped Preston get rid of his briefs, and assisted him in sliding on a condom.

The hammock teetered precariously, threatening to throw them off their unsteady perch. Clementine waited until it steadied, then slowly lifted her hips, closed her hand around him and took him inside.

Preston groaned raggedly, and his hands closed around her breasts. He fondled and massaged, and pulled on her nipples.

Clementine gasped, and she wrapped her legs and knees around him, moving her hips, twisting and clenching around him, until Preston felt consumed by a raging inferno.

The hammock bucked wildly with their movements, and Preston withdrew, then surged into her again, feeling her satiny prison draw on his very life force with inexorable power. They both felt the hammock begin to tip at the same time, and Preston rolled them over before they crashed onto the ground so that he could absorb the brunt of the spill.

Their fall embedded Preston even more deeply into Clementine, and she moaned as spiraling desire took hold of her again, this time sweeping Preston in its raging wake. Tremors shook their bodies as they called each other's names, and they climbed the peak together, and descended in languid, conjoined contentment.

Thirteen

When Preston called a halt in front of the Radcliffe Research Compound the following morning, Clementine gasped.

She had not expected the sight that greeted her.

Along a wide avenue, several types of enclosures and buildings were laid out—for mammals, birds, reptiles—as well as fenced pens and corrals, chain link cages, walled and glass shelters and inviting islands for bears or semiaquatic animals.

The Radcliffe Research Compound was a world onto itself, an animal kingdom in which some species stalked through thickets or foliage, others performed aerial feats in glass cages and still others played in a waterfall gently cascading onto rocks, which displayed yet other species.

"I didn't know this island possessed such a diversity of shrubs, trees and flowers," she whispered.

"It doesn't," Preston said. "Generous donations have enabled the Radcliffe Research Compound to either grow or import flora native to the animals' habitat—to provide cover and privacy from the public, as well as the right type of food for their varied diets." Pointing to a large greenhouse which was set to one side, away from what appeared to be an entire village of free-roaming animals, he added, "Claudio said to meet him there—he's in charge of preparing the special diet of hummingbirds, for one."

"Hummingbirds?" Clementine asked as she kept an eye out for Claudio. They were almost an hour early, since Preston wanted to find the rendezvous point, and make sure no one surprised them.

"Claudio said that hummingbirds had proved difficult to feed, dying in captivity until an English breeder devised the proper formula of condensed milk, baby food, honey and vitamins."

"Why is Claudio willing to help you?"

"Because he loves animals. He'd been asked by someone to look the other way when they wanted to smuggle out some animals, but he refused. He's attending the university on the mainland—right now it's their summer break—and he wants to become a zoo administrator. Claudio loves his charges, and doesn't want anything to jeopardize their survival, which is why he approached me that first day I went into town."

Suddenly alert, Preston stopped talking. Although they were safely out of sight behind some large trees, he didn't want to take any chances.

The noise he'd first heard seemed to be getting louder. Clementine and Preston looked at each other, but didn't move.

Without warning, a large gray tube wrapped itself around Preston's neck.

He raised his machete, thinking a snake had descended on him, when Clementine warned, "Don't, Preston! It's only a baby elephant!"

The affectionate beast removed its long trunk from around Preston, raised it in the air and trumpeted a friendly greeting.

"Shh," Preston told the animal in a loud whisper. "You're going to give us away."

The elephant stretched its trunk and rolled it around the arm Preston had raised to scold him.

"Go away!" Preston said desperately.

Despite their precarious positions, Clementine could not help but laugh.

"Great sense of humor you have," Preston complained as the elephant refused to budge. "Do something."

Clementine tried to push the pachyderm away.

"Oh, brilliant. He only has a couple of tons on you."

"But he's just a baby. He wants to play," Clementine told him as the elephant ran his trunk over Preston's chest, and then concentrated on his head. When the animal tried to slip its trunk into Preston's ear, he slapped it firmly.

"Bad boy," he scolded.

Amazingly, the baby elephant dropped its trunk, letting it droop disconsolately, and slowly ambled away, the picture of dejection.

"You hurt his feelings," Clementine told Preston.

"His feelings can recover," Preston answered. "But if we're discovered by the wrong crowd, we might not."

"Do you think Claudio is on the level?"

"I hope so, but I'm only going on gut instinct. He seemed quite dedicated when he was telling me about the Convention on International Trade in Endangered Species of Wild Fauna and Flora, which according to him every country in South America belongs to."

"Doesn't seem to be doing much good here, though," Clementine told him, keeping an eye out for both Claudio and the cute pachyderm.

"That's because there is still a worldwide demand for caimans and anaconda, as well as animal skins from leopards and ocelots, and ivory from tusked animals. Illegal trade is hard to stop when there is such a huge market."

Impressed by his knowledge, Clementine asked him, "Have you done some investigating on endangered species before?"

Preston nodded, checking his watch. "A few times. A couple of years ago, the paper signed me up to attend what was supposed to be a photographic safari in Africa, but which turned out to be a front for heavy smuggling. And before coming here, I had our research department give me a full dossier on the island, Radcliffe Research included."

"I still can't believe the Radcliffe Compound would be endangering their own economic survival, even if they were to ignore every other ethical or moral rationale," she said, shaking her head. "A blackmail ring operating out of a wildlife conservation refuge?"

"Think of the opportunity for smuggling, especially since the authorities here are more interested in keeping the tourists happy than in controlling the illegal trade in animals. With the police turning a blind eye, drugs could be brought in and distributed, and animals smuggled out and sold on the black market—sort of killing two birds with one stone.''

Clementine caught some movement near the greenhouse, and grabbed Preston's shoulder. "Is that him?" she asked, even as she tried to peek from behind the *ombú*.

"Yeah, that's Claudio," Preston said. "Let's go."

They straightened slowly, feeling their bones creak from the uncomfortable crouch they'd been in for so long.

Clementine remained outside the greenhouse as a lookout while Preston went in and talked to Claudio, who, like many others on the island, spoke excellent English.

Within minutes, the compound began coming to life, and Clementine poked her head in the door. "Someone's coming," she whispered.

She saw Preston try to give Claudio some money, who refused at first. Hearing something about "education," she saw that Claudio finally accepted the money. Then she overheard, *"Tengan mucho cuidado."* Be very careful.

Preston patted Claudio on the back. Then he joined her, grabbing her hand and pulling her into the jungle with him.

They were soon lost in the dense foliage.

"Pay dirt!" Preston said as they picked up their backpacks, hidden a short distance away in some thick bushes. "I've just discovered that they're holding my uncle, unharmed."

They traveled in silence for a couple of hours, trying to put as much distance as possible between the compound and themselves.

As they reached the small, sparkling stream where they'd had a quick rest the day before, Preston dropped to the ground and took out his canteen. "Let's take a breather, and then we'll make tracks back to the Puerco Loco."

Clementine smiled, always amused when she heard the name of their resort, since it didn't fit the elegance of the place.

Preston looked at her questioningly, and she told him, "The name, Puerco Loco. It means crazy swine."

"Crazy pig?"

"Apparently the island was originally overrun with wild boar, but they were eliminated when tourism became a thriving business. The developer of the resort thought it would be amusing, as well as historically accurate."

After drinking some water, Clementine washed her perspiring face in the cool, gurgling brook.

Looking at her watch, she said, "We don't have much time. My mother is getting divorced this afternoon—provided Ronald finally made his appearance—and I want to be there."

Preston's eyes narrowed. "You don't sound too concerned about my uncle."

Clementine colored guiltily.

"You really don't believe in his innocence, do you?" Preston demanded. "If you recall, he was supposed to be getting divorced today alongside your mother."

Clementine looked at his handsome face, and felt pain at the disappearance of those sexy dimples, which had been in such abundant evidence last night. But she couldn't lie. She still believed Ford's vanishing act had been engineered by some hidden agenda of his own. She believed in Preston's innocence—her heart told her that the man who had made such exquisite love to her last night and into the morning would not...*could not* hurt her.

But Clementine had found that real life operated differently than fiction. In a book, the most likely suspect could always be dismissed...mysteries were not supposed to be too obvious...

In real life, when clues pointed to a certain person, that person was usually the culprit. Police were often fond of saying that most murders were committed by a loved one, someone close to the victim.

Preston was being blinded by his love for his uncle.

"I know that you and your uncle are very close, with your being an only child, and Ford your father's only sibling and so close to your own age. But as I said earlier, he could be in need of money—"

"He would have asked my folks for help. My parents are quite wealthy in their own right."

"I'm sorry, Preston. As a private investigator—"

"You're far more than that now, and you know it," he said harshly. "If you care about me, you have to care about my uncle." Preston put his canteen away and stood. "And if I say he is innocent, that should be good enough for you."

He waited for Clementine to say the words, but as much as she wanted to, she could not give him the reassurance he sought.

"Well, I'd hoped to be spared this mistrust of yours, but I guess you don't operate on faith alone, do you? As Celeste implied, you believe half the world is guilty of screwing the other half." Slipping on his backpack, he added, "I had the research department of my paper do some digging into patrons of the Radcliffe Compound, and the information should be waiting for me at the resort."

Clementine opened her mouth to defend herself against his unjust condemnation, but Preston forestalled her. "You might just want to consider that another player has entered the game. Someone who will also be getting divorced—and no, not Ford," Preston said, his tone hard, his eyes accusing.

"Delores?" Clementine asked as she put her water flask in her backpack, thinking that aside from Ronald, only Delores had been missing from the divorce roster for the week. Clementine had checked with the chapel director as soon as she'd begun to get suspicious.

And Ford's soon-to-be-ex-wife—provided Ford made an appearance himself—had conveniently been delayed twice. Urgent business to take care of first?

Stalking off in the direction of the Puerco Loco, Preston said over his shoulder, "No, a bit closer to home. Try Ronald Beinor."

In the trek that followed, which was filled with hostile silence, Clementine had time to ponder Preston's last words. But she could not reconcile her view of harmless Ronald with Preston's accusation. Also, she realized that although she had disliked her mother's husband for so long—and would love to see him thrown in jail—she was trying to give him the benefit of the doubt and avoid letting a personal antipathy cloud her professional judgment.

On the other hand, if this were a plot in a mystery novel, Ronald would be the least likely suspect, she told herself. Of course, a woman—Delores—would be even less suspect, she told herself staunchly.

Although Clementine knew Celeste's love for Ronald had died, she also knew that her mother retained some fondness for the man. They had been together three years, after all, and in the beginning, they had both appeared to be very much in love.

Shaking her head, Clementine picked up her pace. Since they had left the hammocks in a hiding place near the compound, she found the going much easier. This time she did not offer to wield the machete, knowing that Preston would not have accepted her suggestion. They more or less followed the path they had taken yesterday, but Preston took a few detours in case anyone had tried to track them down.

Her thoughts returned to Preston's last statement.

Could it be that she was too close to the scene, too intimately involved?

Could Ronald be the silent partner, and she too blind to see?

As the resort came into view, Clementine promised herself she would be doubly vigilant. Preston was an astute investigator in his own right: if he was correct, and she was wrong, Ford's safety could hang in the balance.

Seven divorces were scheduled for that afternoon.

Although Clementine had told Preston that she would understand if he did not attend the Cahill/Beinor proceedings, and continued looking for Ford,

Preston insisted on coming. He was hoping he could learn something about Ford's disappearance before confronting Ronald, since his office had still not faxed him the information he'd requested.

Whatever his reasons, Clementine was glad Preston was at the Capilla del Mar.

The setting was breathtaking.

The *capilla* was a white building with pillars and marble steps, and flowers abounded. Several of the resort guests had stopped by to view the ceremonies, everyone dressed in romantic-looking clothes.

A band in the background was playing love ballads, alternating them with poignant tangos and soothing instrumentals.

Clementine smoothed the skirt of her ruffled halter dress. She had changed from her original selection, a softly tailored suit, since she knew Preston would be attending.

Looking at him now, in his dark gray slacks and pearl gray buccaneer shirt, open at the neck, the silky material flowing, the sleeves billowing in the breeze, Clementine reflected that Preston could very well have been a pirate in another life.

As Preston stood with his back to the sea, his eyes on the waterfall framed by the mountains, which rose against a diaphanous sky, she felt her breath catch.

His hair, wavy, curling around his collar, was ensnared by the wind and shone like antique gold. His eyes gleamed like polished silver, and his stance, proud shoulders back, arms clasped behind him, threw into relief his powerful, solidly muscled body.

Clementine missed the closeness they'd shared the night before. Today, his responses to her had been curt, and she could not really blame him.

The wind began to pick up a little, and the French braid that Clementine had threaded with an aqua ribbon to match her dress tickled against her bare back.

Tearing her gaze away from Preston, Clementine looked toward the chapel to see if Celeste and Ronald had arrived.

Ronald had gotten to the resort two hours ago, profusely apologizing to Celeste, offering an excuse regarding a last-minute deal, and was now getting ready. He had thanked Clementine for keeping Celeste company, and for making new arrangements when he'd missed the first scheduled ceremony. Celeste had neither rebuked Ronald for his lateness, nor had she told him that he had almost been a part of a double divorce.

Preston had insisted that he and Clementine go to the Capilla del Mar before Celeste and Ronald. He did not want Ronald to suspect that Preston was onto him.

Celeste had been told of the latest developments, and sworn to secrecy. Although Celeste was not convinced of Ronald's involvement, she had agreed to keep Preston's suspicions to herself.

Clementine had come to realize how much Preston cared for her mother. She had come to see how concerned he was about Celeste's welfare—despite their short acquaintance—and she felt like a perfect heel for doubting Ford.

"That's a beautiful necklace."

The deep voice startled Clementine. Her hands flew to her neck, where a necklace of alternating diamonds and aquamarines in the shape of a star shone.

"The necklace and matching earrings are a present from my mother," Clementine said, her eyes searching his.

Preston's gaze softened for a minute as it rested on her bare shoulders and the slight cleavage revealed by the ruffly neckline of her dress.

His hand rose slowly, hesitantly, caressing her arm, then her shoulder with a featherlike touch. His fingers traveled upward, circling her neck to brush against her hair. "Your hair looks like a flame. Do you think it will consume me?" he murmured to himself.

Lips parted, eyes half-closed, Clementine leaned into Preston. He twirled her, and pulled her against his body, his hands closing around her waist, his thighs molding against her derriere.

She leaned against him, breathing in the totally male scent of him, tropical, lemony, clean, intoxicating, and reveling in the strength of his chest and arms.

Preston buried his face in her hair, smelling the exotic fragrances of the island in the flowing braid. Then he slanted his face downward, depositing a tiny rosary of kisses against the velvety skin of her neck.

As Clementine became lost in the enchantment of his touch, she felt Preston stiffen against her.

Preston saw the tall, fair-haired man accompanying Celeste, and asked Clementine, "Did you ever wonder why that man in white you saw enter the resort looked so familiar to you?"

Puzzled, Clementine followed his gaze, and saw Celeste's petite form protectively enclosed in Ronald's embrace.

Ronald was tall, muscular—and blond.

He was dressed in a dark suit, which enhanced his good looks. His hair was cut shorter than usual, and Clementine realized that—and the fact she had never seen Ronald in white before—had been one of the reasons she had never made the connection.

Moving away from Preston and walking slowly to her mother's side, Clementine told herself that she had indeed been too close to this situation. But she was certainly going to keep her eyes wide open now.

Preston followed Clementine, putting his arm around her waist again, and schooled his features into impassivity.

Fourteen

The ceremonies were performed beautifully.

The seven couples looked radiant. Ranging in ages from twenty to seventy, they left the onlooker wondering.

Why were they divorcing? They all seemed perfect fits.

But, as the minister had solemnly intoned, these couples were ending their relationships in the spirit with which they had begun them: with hope and affection, if not the untarnished first bloom of love.

These couples wanted to remain friends, and not become bitter enemies.

For some, children were involved. For those who had no children, the couples felt the time they had invested had not been a total loss or hardship.

They preferred to end things in a civilized manner, and endeavor to remember only the good times.

"Quite a winning philosophy," Clementine murmured.

"Too bad it doesn't work out that way for every couple," Preston said in a low tone. "For some, friendship is no longer a possibility."

Following his gaze, Clementine frowned. She hoped Preston was not referring to their own relationship.

Ronald, looking very much like a man in love as he kept an arm around Celeste while the ceremony came to a close, struck her more like a debonair con man than the cold-blooded ringleader of a smuggling and blackmail operation. But obviously, he had to have more depth than he evinced, or her mother would not have fallen for him.

The more she thought about it, the more she realized that there was a lot going on beneath all that surface charm. Ronald, with his blond good looks . . .

And it would be just like him to hold out a carrot, have Clementine follow him while his confederate made a clean getaway.

Knowing she would never, in a million years, suspect suave Ronald Beinor.

Who had yet to get to the island, scheduled to arrive a couple of days after Celeste.

But had he arrived late?

Or had he claimed some pressing matters back in the States so that he could in fact get here ahead of Celeste? Knowing that Clementine was going to be witnessing the divorce, maybe Ronald had felt he would be safer if he set up his plans *before* Clementine arrived.

Still, Ronald?

The strains of the song "We've Only Just Begun" penetrated Clementine's consciousness, and she realized Preston was saying something to her.

"Do you think you can keep Ronald occupied for a while?"

Before tearing her gaze away from Celeste and Ronald, who were having their picture taken in a gazebo overgrown with multicolored flowers, she smiled at them and waved.

"What are you up to?" she asked Preston.

"I want to go through Ronald's things."

"Like his passport, to see when he actually arrived?" Clementine asked. Preston's eyebrows shot skyward. "If he really is the mastermind behind the smuggling and blackmail, do you think he would actually leave any incriminating evidence behind?"

Preston pulled her against him.

"Are you actually beginning to see him as a suspect?"

Clementine looked up at him, her smile intact, her eyes stormy. "I've always considered him a suspect—I don't discount anyone's involvement until I have proof."

"Guilty until proven innocent?" Preston asked against her mouth.

His lips, so close and tempting, did not distract Clementine from his true purpose. Preston was trying to throw Ronald off the scent—and she was not entirely averse to cooperating in such a noble cause.

Winding her arms around Preston's neck, Clementine gave him a kiss that left him breathless.

He came up for air, and then bent his head to come back for more.

Smiling, Clementine reminded him, "Ronald's room, remember? B and E?"

His eyes turned the slate gray of a thundercloud, and he mouthed, "Later," before claiming her mouth again with a brief, hard kiss that promised a lot more.

Breathless, she watched him stride away, and moved toward the gazebo.

"Clementine, sweetheart. How nice of you to come down to Isla Gaucha with your mother. It was unfortunate that business kept me away from Celeste for so long."

"I understand you were vehemently opposed to Mother's coming to Isla Gaucha."

Ronald's eyes flashed, but just for an instant. It was long enough, though, for Clementine to realize he was annoyed.

Could he really have fooled her all this time with his polished, wastrel-about-town act?

"I was against the divorce, yes. Celeste knows I still love her very much."

"I guess my mother didn't realize that, since you've been gone so often and for so long, especially during the past year."

Ronald's eyes narrowed, although he retained his pleasant smile. "It's true, I've been guilty of neglecting Celeste, but I hope she will give me another chance."

Startled, Clementine looked at her mother, who regarded both of them with a tranquil expression. "We'll see, Ronald. I think it would be best if we spent some time away from each other, don't you? That way we can reflect on our relationship, and decide what future course of action to take."

Clementine grinned inwardly. Her mother *was* grace under pressure. Ronald didn't look happy at Celeste's answer, but he couldn't very well argue with her reasonable, serene statement.

Knowing that she had to buy Preston some time, Clementine slipped into the role that Ronald would recognize.

"I must say, Ronald, I've never been so glad to see you...now that you and Mother are finally divorced."

His smile was that of a patient, indulgent father.

Hindsight was always twenty-twenty, Clementine told herself, even as she kept her own smile plastered on her face. She had never bothered to hide her disapproval of Ronald, but knew he had always taken it as a daughter's not considering any suitor or husband worthy of her mother—nor an equal to her father.

Not in a million years would Ronald Beinor equal Sterling Cahill—even if Ronald were not a criminal.

The last doubt was finally gone. Even if Ronald had made it to the island on a private plane or boat, leaving no trace; even if Preston didn't find anything incriminating in Ronald's room, or Preston's office was not able to connect Ronald to the Radcliffe Research Compound, Clementine was convinced that Ford was innocent and Ronald was not.

Hopefully, Ronald hadn't done anything irreparable yet. For, if he had been on the island all this time, he must have known of Celeste's growing attraction to Ford. Ronald was a very possessive man...and it was obvious he was still crazy about Celeste.

While relieved on the one hand that her mother would come to no harm, on the other, Clementine worried about Preston's uncle.

Who knew what Ronald—the *real* Ronald, the one he'd camouflaged so cleverly for the past few years—was capable of? Clementine needed to get to Preston, fast!

Noticing that her mother was regarding her with well-concealed concern, Clementine told Ronald, "Since this is sort of a goodbye party, I hope you don't mind if I join you at tonight's banquet."

"Leaving us so soon?" Ronald asked, his eyes glittering.

"Peter told me one of my cases requires my immediate presence, so I have to cut my vacation short."

"Oh, sorry to hear that, Tweetie," Celeste said with the proper amount of regret, her glance openly questioning.

Clementine hugged her mother, and whispered in her ear, "Don't worry. Everything's under control."

Celeste hugged her daughter, hard. "Take care," she whispered.

Clementine started walking away, but Ronald's voice stopped her. "Clementine, will you be bringing that young man I saw you with?"

"Preston?" Clementine asked casually. When Ronald nodded, she shrugged her shoulders. "I don't know what his plans are, but I'll certainly convey your invitation."

"Please do. I'd like to buy you two lovebirds dinner."

Later that evening, Clementine and Preston put in an appearance.

The banquet was sumptuous, and the music festive and loud.

Preston had told Clementine on their way to the dining room that he had found nothing incriminating in Ronald's room—not even a passport.

Which meant that Ronald either had it with him, or was keeping it in a secure place, like the hotel safe.

Clementine had never known Ronald to be that careful or to plan ahead for any eventualities.

At least, the Ronald she'd known.

Or the Ronald she'd been allowed to see.

The research department of Preston's paper had shed some light on Ronald Beinor: he was one of the benefactors of Radcliffe Research, which meant he was trusted, and had easy access to the compound.

Clementine wasn't sure how the blackmail tied into everything, but she was determined to find out.

She recalled that Ronald had met Celeste on a Caribbean singles cruise, and had swept her mother off her feet.

Celeste had behaved uncharacteristically, and married Ronald in Florida, as soon as the ship had come into port.

Hurt at the time for not having been invited to the wedding, Clementine had nevertheless been happy for her mother, hoping that she had finally found the man who could make her forget Sterling Cahill.

That happiness changed to guarded optimism when she'd first met Ronald Beinor, and later to resignation.

She realized now that Ronald had never known about Clementine's occupation when he met and married Celeste. She had considered him a gigolo, but apparently Ronald was a lot more.

"Don't worry so much," Preston told her, dropping a kiss on her forehead to erase the tension lines he saw there. "At least we know Ronald hasn't killed Ford yet—a friend of Claudio's told me a short while ago he's been moved from his original hiding place to the compound."

"Preston, I'm so sorry—"

He cut her words off with a gentle kiss, and said, "Just keep your chin up. We won't stay too long."

As soon as dinner was over, Clementine excused herself from her mother.

"Mother, don't bother to wait up. Preston and I are going to do the town tonight. It's my last chance before I leave."

Celeste's smile hid the quick fear that had shown in her big blue eyes. "I'm glad you're finally having some fun. That's why I talked you into coming in the first place."

"I intend to show your daughter a great time, Celeste." To Ronald, he said, "Thank you for dinner."

"Anytime," Ronald answered, his eyes laserlike as they went from Clementine to Preston.

Clementine smiled at both her mother and Ronald, and picked up her evening purse.

"Good night. See you in the morning."

Fifteen

Within the hour, Clementine and Preston were back on the road to the Radcliffe Research Compound.

Clementine apologized to Preston once more, concerned about Ford's fate, and he told her to forget it.

"You were too close to them, and after meeting Ronald, I can see how he could have pulled the wool over your eyes. If he was able to fool Celeste for three years, he must be a hell of an actor."

"I think he really cares for my mother."

"I think so, too," Preston agreed. "Very few people are totally evil—Celeste just happens to be Ronald's soft spot."

"Thank God he has one," Clementine said as Preston trained a powerful flashlight on a particularly dense part of the trail. Because they had not wanted anyone to follow them, or anticipate the direction from which they were coming, they had taken another route. It was taking them longer to reach their destination and the going was even rougher than the last time. They were exhausted.

"One down, one to go," Preston told her as he rounded a tree with immense roots.

When she looked at him, puzzled, Preston explained, "Divorces. Delores finally came in tonight. She left a message for me when she couldn't find Ford. Apparently, she couldn't resist Calle Florida in Buenos Aires—she wanted one last shopping spree on the house."

"Ford will be thrilled," Clementine said.

"You'd be surprised. Ford is a generous guy, and—"

Preston stopped suddenly in front of her.

Instinctively swallowing a cry of surprise, Clementine barely avoided running into Preston. The faint breeze that managed to penetrate the thick growth carried human sounds on its slender wings.

Preston's arm curved around her shoulders, and he pulled her protectively against him.

Parallel to the route they were taking, voices could be heard. The men on the way to the compound must have already cleared a path, because Preston and Clementine did not detect the harsh sound of a machete chopping against the dense vegetation.

The loud voices traveled easily in the jungle night, which meant the men were not far.

Preston raised his flashlight to study her expression. And he read on her face the same idea that had crossed his mind.

"Shall we follow them?"

"Beats hard labor," Clementine answered.

Keeping the flashlight low on the ground so they could not be seen, Preston and Clementine waited until the sounds became even fainter. Even though the other men were not making any attempt to be quiet, it was better to err on the side of caution.

Clementine and Preston made their way to the well-worn trail in a few minutes, the light wind dissipating the night's heat from their sweaty skin.

Preston slid his machete in the back of his khaki pants, and Clementine took the time to check her gun.

"Luckily, they don't expect anyone to follow them. We should be able to make good time."

Clementine nodded. "Let's go."

Preston and Clementine arrived at the Radcliffe Research Compound two hours later.

Light was already dusting the horizon with a golden tinge. They crept closer to the compound, trying to determine how many men they would have to contend with.

While there had been nothing in the men's behavior to incriminate them, their using the cover of night to travel was suspicious.

Since they had been forced to keep their distance, Clementine and Preston had not been able to identify the three men, and had decided to play it safe.

As they rested by a small pool, Preston sat down to drink some water.

Feeling something foreign on his arm, he looked down and almost jumped out of his skin.

As it was, his catapulting off the rock he'd been sitting on robbed Clementine of ten years of her life.

Luckily, she was able to clap her hand against Preston's mouth, and stop the loud curses about to erupt.

"You do have a way with animals," she told him, unable to keep the laughter from her voice. "You even attract the lowly bloodsuckers. Did you happen to know they contain both male and female reproductive organs?"

"If you don't get this parasite off me this instant, not only will it start to breed, but you will have a man faint dead away at your feet."

She considered his words. "Well, that does have certain possibilities—"

"Clem!"

"All right, all right," Clementine said soothingly, proceeding to remove the leech from Preston's arm.

"Aren't you going to kill it?" Preston demanded.

"Of course not. This one is a medicinal leech."

"Oh, and that makes a difference?" he asked with ill-disguised disgust.

"Naturally. Until very recently, this type of leech was used to help heal bruises and cure diseases by removing bad blood. Now they're still used in medical research because they produce hirudin, an element that prevents blood clotting."

"Next you're going to tell me they are an endangered species," Preston said, shaking his head in disbelief.

"They are," she said as she disposed of the leech. "This type of leech is almost extinct in Europe."

"My heart bleeds for them," Preston told her dryly. "No pun intended."

About to answer him, Clementine caught movement out of her peripheral vision.

The same three men who had preceded them into Radcliffe Research were walking toward a truck parked at the edge of the compound. They were carrying some animals.

Their furtive looks and stealthy movements did not proclaim them trusted veterinarians of Radcliffe Research.

As they neared the truck, Clementine grabbed Preston's arm.

"Do you recognize any of the animals?"

"The golden lion tamarin," Preston said grimly. "That type of marmoset was in the news recently. They're in danger of being wiped out since they occupy a small area of a nature preserve in Brazil that was being threatened by wildfire."

His eyes narrowing, Preston muttered under his breath, "And what is that guy doing with two of them?"

"It's best to keep them in pairs," Clementine said. "In large groups, biting matches between two adults can result in the death of the subordinate. These two must be of the same sex, and familiar with each other."

"Too bad they don't inflict some painful bites on the jerk carrying them," Preston said.

As the beautiful animals were put in a cage, Clementine said, "It's a shame what people will do for money. With those shimmering, yellow-gold coats and mane, those monkeys are one of the most brightly colored members of the animal kingdom, and therefore in high demand."

One of the other men opened the sack he was carrying and took out a small, dark, wriggling object. Clementine gasped, "That's a spectacled cub."

"A what?" Preston asked, craning his neck to get a better look.

"It's the only species of bear native to Latin America. It's sparsely distributed in certain parts of the Andes, and it's prized for both its fur and flesh."

Preston noticed the white facial markings and said, "It almost looks like a raccoon."

"Cuter," Clementine said, her wrath fully aroused. "They have the slimmest chances of survival in the wild, and with these monsters, who knows what will happen to them."

"First things first," Preston reminded her, placing a comforting arm around her. "After we find Ford, I'll help you nail these creeps."

Hearing the fear for his uncle in Preston's voice, Clementine gave him a quick kiss. "Don't worry. We'll rescue Ford. Then these thugs will see what being helpless feels like."

The third man put the baby ocelot he was carrying in the back of the truck, and Clementine tensed. "When they began running out of jaguars to make fur coats, they started on the ocelots. Since they are only about half the size, twice as many are needed to make a 'good' coat."

"We'll get them back," Preston promised.

She nodded, and brought her mind forcibly to the problem at hand. "We have to try to figure out where they might have put your uncle. In the limited time we have, we can't possibly cover every building or enclosure."

"I picked up a visitor's guide at the resort. The guidebook has a map of the compound," Preston said. They both pored over the listings, and tried to pick out the largest structures.

"Well, I think we can narrow the possibilities to the Feline Kingdom, the Golden Eagle Castle and the

Monkey Island. They seem to be the likeliest locations."

"I'll take the castle," Preston said. "It contains a waterfall, pool and trees and flowers. It would be easy to hide someone there."

As Preston was ready to move out, Clementine held him back. "Wait! We need a diversion."

Some keepers began to emerge from the main lodge.

Clementine told Preston, "At some zoos, animals like giraffes and zebras spend the night indoors, where they can be safe, and where the vets and caretakers can examine them."

"So?" Preston asked impatiently.

"So when the keepers want them to return to their stalls, they use whistles like the kind sports officials have. And since Grant's zebras, giraffes and ostriches share an area in the wild—"

"They respond to the whistle in unison?" Preston finished, smiling.

Clementine smiled back. "The honest workers of this place are not going to be grateful to us when we cause a stampede...."

"We'll help them sort everything out later," Preston promised. "Ready?"

"We don't have a whistle," she said, but was drowned out by a shrill sound that any sports official would have envied.

It cut through the stillness of the morning with the stridency of a locomotive.

Within seconds, pandemonium broke out.

As the giraffes, zebras and ostriches, conditioned to the whistle, began a mass exodus, several other startled animals emerged.

The three men jumped into the truck, but were stranded as the vehicle was soon engulfed in a sea of different species.

Keepers and volunteers also poured out of the main lodge and perimeter outbuildings, and Preston and Clementine used the cover of confusion to begin their search.

Unfortunately, they had not counted on being swallowed up in the mayhem themselves.

When they tried to make their way to the feline and eagles enclosures, a herd of zebras trooped their way. Preston grabbed Clementine's hand, and they both put their track experience to good use as they sprinted toward safe ground.

But an oversize ostrich and rhinoceros, which looked ready for a triathlon, had other ideas.

"We've attracted a following," Clementine panted, alarmed.

"I thought the idea was to get the *crooks* running for their lives," Preston gasped, narrowly avoiding the baby elephant that had been so enamored of him, and that was now extending its trunk to grab Preston as he flew past.

"That . . . was . . . the . . . general . . . idea," Clementine wheezed. She glanced back and saw that they had not lost their unexpected escorts.

Turning his speed up a notch, Preston almost tore Clementine's arm out of its socket as he pulled her along.

"I thought rhinos were supposed to have bad eyesight," he complained as he spied the horn aimed directly at his backside.

"They do," she concurred, feeling her chest burn from oxygen deprivation. "That's why they charge objects they don't recognize."

"You'd better look out, Clem," Preston warned as he ventured a quick look behind him. "An ostrich seems enchanted with your bottom—and it's gaining on you."

"Unfortunately, ostriches are very curious," Clementine wheezed. "There must be something about my outfit that attracted it."

"We'd better split up," Preston yelled over the pandemonium. "We'll meet back at the place where we came in."

Clementine uttered a strangled, "Agreed," and squeezed Preston's hand before letting go.

Without Clementine to impede his speed, Preston took off as if shot by a cannon.

Clementine was also able to dodge the animals and objects in her path more easily. With a final burst of speed, she eluded the angry-looking ostrich as she vaulted over a fence that enclosed a petting zoo.

Knowing that ostriches looked cute and harmless with those ridiculously long eyelashes, skinny necks and ungainly bodies, but packed a mean wallop in their feet and claws, she swallowed huge gulps of air, relieved.

The ostrich looked positively peeved that its human prey had gotten away. Not wanting to test the leaping ability of a frustrated ostrich, Clementine moved quickly out of harm's way.

A few minutes later, Clementine entered the lion and tiger house with stealth and trepidation.

She should have given Preston the honor of visiting the Feline Kingdom.

Being attacked by an evil ostrich and then eaten by irate tigers was not her idea of a day at the zoo.

A horrible thought occurred to her. What if they'd put Ford in one of the cages of these decidedly hungry-looking animals?

Swallowing past the huge lump of dread in her throat, Clementine squared her shoulders and prepared to enter the lion's den. Literally.

Until a voice, quite close, stopped her dead in her tracks.

"Well, well. What have we here? Dropping in for a visit?"

Sixteen

Clementine swung around, her hand going to the gun she'd slipped into the waistband of her shorts.

"Don't, Clemmie," Ronald advised, his own weapon glinting in the sunlight that streamed through the high skylight.

Clementine froze, her mind still finding it difficult to reconcile the hard-eyed man in front of her with her mother's charming, lightweight ex-husband.

"I'd have thought you and your boyfriend would have gone to the police," Ronald said, coming toward her and extending his hand.

She retreated. "Now, Clemmie," Ronald said, his teeth gleaming like a shark's. "Let's not play games."

Clementine continued backing up until the reinforced glass behind her stopped her progress. "We knew some of the police were involved—we couldn't take the chance on contacting one of the lackeys on your payroll.''

"That rumor served me well," Ronald said, satisfaction in his voice. "It certainly prevented many people from procuring assistance from the local law enforcement. But, as a matter of fact, the police are not in cahoots—they are just underpaid and overworked, and in some cases, incompetent, just like back home.''

He stepped even closer. "I'd like that gun, please," Ronald demanded, an edge of steel in his tone. It was hard to believe that she could ever have taken this man for a weakling. He merited an Oscar.

Trying to buy time, she asked, "How were you able to operate a smuggling ring out of one of the most respected animal centers in the world?''

"Postponing the inevitable, my dear?" Ronald smiled knowingly. "That's all right. I suppose every condemned person deserves to have their questions answered.''

Keeping his gun trained on her, Ronald said, "As I'm sure your reporter friend has found out by now, I have made some generous donations to Radcliffe Research. It's amazing how trusting people become when you're a benefactor. I practically have the run of the place, and I was able to place some of my men in key positions—including administration and transportation.''

"So that you can intercept shipments before they are even recorded.''

"I always said you were smart, my dear. Too smart for your own good. We, of course, don't stop every endangered animal from coming in—but we do appropriate a modest few, which we then sell to interested parties . . . and no one the wiser. Since the center is more interested in the rescue of animals and research, it didn't spend too much time or money safeguarding accounting procedures. Also, volunteer help and workers at minimum wages are hard to find. Needless to say, my donations are measly change compared to the money billionaires are willing to pay for, say, a tamarin.''

Despite her precarious situation, Clementine was enraged. "How can you do that to helpless animals, creatures that are in danger of dying out?''

"I'm only interested in my own death, Clemmie. What do I care what's left on this earth when I'm no longer here?''

"And the blackmail?'' Clementine asked quickly as Ronald advanced once again.

"Oh, you heard about that? Well, I suppose it was bound to come out sooner or later.'' He shrugged philosophically. "That was merely a sideline. When high-level executives with nose-candy problems arrived for easy divorces, I made sure to leave some *presents* in their rooms. Then one of my men, impersonating the police, would arrest them. I would then step in, offering to intercede with the authorities, and provide a way out that involved no publicity.''

"And they paid you.''

"Of course, my dear. But although the money was nothing to sneeze at, the real reason behind the blackmail was to have something to hold over their heads, should I need any favors in the future.''

Surreptitiously looking around for a way out, Clementine said, "Your own little empire.''

Ronald grinned. "Quite clever, wouldn't you say? And now that I've satisfied your curiosity, may I have the gun?"

Hanging her head in a defeated attitude, Clementine moved her hand to give him the gun.

"Slowly, Clemmie. I know you don't give up easily, so don't think you can pull a fast one on me."

About to make her move, Clementine froze as two goons burst through the doorway. They looked from Ronald to Clementine, and the shorter man told Ronald, "We can't find Kilpatrick."

Like a snake, Ronald whipped around. "Texas, you fool! He's looking for his uncle. Just make sure you're there to surprise Kilpatrick when he attempts his heroic rescue."

Clementine recognized the man's southwestern accent as the one she'd overheard during her walk in the jungle that first day, the one who'd gotten away while Ronald had tricked her into following him.

Recalling the many arguments she'd had with Preston debating Ronald's innocence and Ford's apparent guilt, Clementine hoped she was not too late to save Ford—and to save Preston, who would be walking into a trap.

The two men left, and Ronald said softly, "I'm still waiting for your gun, Clementine."

Reluctantly, she handed it over to him.

"Smart move. At least it prolongs your existence for a little while." Shaking his head, he said sorrowfully, "If only you would have just enjoyed your vacation..."

"What about Ford?"

"Ford Kilpatrick? I had a nice stash ready to be conveniently discovered in his room. Only this time, I would have called the police, and had him arrested. I didn't like the way he was cozying up to my wife."

"*Ex*-wife," Clementine reminded him.

"Not for long. Once Celeste loses her beloved daughter, as well as her two new friends, she'll be quite desolate, don't you think? And I'll be right there to console her."

The blood froze in Clementine's veins. "You're a monster," she whispered, fear and loathing rusting her voice.

"Don't worry. I'll take good care of Celeste." Directing Clementine to move with a flick of his gun, Ronald threw the other weapon into one of the cages. Immediately, a leopard cub came over and began sniffing it.

"Ronald, you can't leave the gun there. One of the animals could injure itself."

Genuinely amused, Ronald said, "Clemmie, you're something else. Now you're a champion of animal rights, too?"

"Why hurt something when you don't have to," she reasoned. Crossing her arms, she said, "I am not moving until I get that gun out of there."

"Well, I can't kill you here. You still could prove useful in smoking Kilpatrick out." Regarding her thoughtfully, he said, "Besides, you're right. That's a beautiful animal. And since I'm going to close up shop here permanently—thanks to you and the Kilpatricks, a bit sooner than planned—I might as well take anything I can get. So go in there and get me that cub." He threw her the master key, which Clementine caught easily on the fly.

When Clementine didn't move, Ronald waved the gun impatiently. "Come on. All hell's broken loose, and I have to get ready to break camp."

Clementine opened the door as directed, and walked over to where the gun lay. "The cub, Clemmie, the cub. Not the gun. Please."

With a disgusted look over her shoulder, Clementine headed for the cub.

And halted in her tracks when mama leopard put in an appearance with another beautiful cub in tow.

"Don't worry about it, Clemmie. I've got you covered."

The mother leopard, sensing danger, growled threateningly.

The chubby, clumsy cub went to join its sibling, and they both began a rolling, biting choreography.

It would have been an adorable scene had Ronald not loomed behind her with that lethal weapon.

"Ronald, don't," Clementine said, afraid for the animal who was only acting out of normal maternal instinct. "I think I can get the cub. You don't have to kill the mother."

"Better not take any chances," Ronald said, aiming at the adult leopard. "I'll just remove the danger right now, and you can bring me both cubs."

"No!" Clementine yelled, throwing herself at Ronald, not able to stand the thought of such a beautiful, noble animal being destroyed just because it was trying to protect its young.

Startled, Ronald fired the gun, and out of the corner of her eye, Clementine saw the mother leopard crumble.

Clementine landed on Ronald, and they both fell to the floor, Ronald on the bottom, the wind knocked out of him.

Springing to her feet, Clementine aimed a measured kick against Ronald's head, and he lay inert.

After confirming that Ronald was only unconscious, and not dead, she picked up her gun and went to check on the adult leopard.

The cubs were issuing baby growls and climbing over the mother, licking its face gently. Clementine pushed the cubs away and monitored the animal's breathing.

The leopard was still alive.

Running outside, Clementine chased a keeper down. She explained the situation, telling him to call the police, tie up Ronald Beinor and make sure the leopard was looked after.

Then she went in search of Preston and Ford.

As she approached the Primate House, Clementine noticed two men in the brown-and-gold uniforms of Radcliffe Research who were making no attempt to corral wayward animals. They were not the Texan and the redheaded giant who had come into the Feline Kingdom, but two men whose stealthy actions in the midst of chaos caught her attention.

Ronald needed several men to operate his smuggling and blackmailing rings. These were probably two of them. Following her hunch, Clementine shadowed them.

She plastered herself against the side of the huge building, and drew her gun.

Suddenly an arm snaked around her throat, and a hand covered her mouth.

About to kick backward and throw her assailant over her shoulder, Clementine recognized the voice of the man whispering, "Clem," in her ear.

She relaxed against the hard, warm body, and slowly turned.

"What happened to you?" she asked.

"I took care of one of those goons who stole the spectacled bears and company," Preston told her. Pointing to the building with his head, he added, "He and three buddies were transferring Ford to the Primate House from one of the outbuildings, and he noticed me following."

"Then let's go in and get your uncle."

"Hold on," Preston said, grabbing Clementine's arm as she prepared to go into the Primate House. "There are at least four people there."

"So?" Clementine waved her weapon. "We've got the great equalizers."

"Too dangerous. Let's create a distraction, and even out the odds."

"Not another distraction," Clementine groaned. "I was almost trampled under the last one. Besides, the police are on their way—they're not involved in this mess. And I've already taken care of Ronald," she informed him. "I think we can deal with the men inside."

"But they might kill Ford before we can rescue him."

Clementine thought for a moment, then brightened.

"I've still got the master key Ronald gave me. I'm going to let some of the animals out.... That ought to create a cover for you so you can get Ford out safely."

Before Preston could say anything, Clementine took off at a run.

The compound was still in an uproar. Keepers, vets, volunteers—they were all trying to round up the wandering animals.

Noticing some very friendly-looking baby elephants, rhinos and giraffes, Clementine approached a keeper and asked for his help. The man contacted two more keepers, and they began leading their charges toward the Primate House, picking up a few curious ostriches and vicuñas along the way.

Clementine, in the meantime, snuck into the Primate House through a side door. Walking by the cages of some gorillas, she noticed a computer in a small office. The compound appeared to be in the last transition stage from manual to electronic controls. She could just open some of the cage doors from the control room, which would be safer.

Knowing that Preston would use the distraction provided by the keepers and their charges, Clementine let some of the primates out.

Within seconds, there were scared screams and vicious curses turning the air blue. Two of the men flew by her, gorillas and orangutans in hot pursuit. Outside, they were met by a caravan of keepers and assorted animals.

Holding her gun against her chest with both hands, Clementine left the control center.

Slightly ahead of her, on the other side of the building, she saw Preston enter. He didn't notice the two men who left an adjacent room and snuck up behind him.

Checking both sides before sprinting, Clementine let the gun drop to her side and made it to the room just as she heard the unmistakable sound of flesh on flesh.

The two men tailing Preston had obviously surprised him as he was trying to untie his uncle. A ruffian was lying unconscious on the floor, but another of the thugs had Preston's arms pinned behind him, while a third alternated his blows from midsection to face and back again.

Coolly aiming her gun at the thug who was doing the punching, Clementine called out, "Gentlemen, gentlemen, where has your sense of fair play gone?"

The man who'd been beating Preston turned around. She recognized the muscle-bound bully as one of the men who had talked to Preston the day she'd followed him to town. Ronald had certainly covered all bases.

The second man, the one who had been holding Preston, released him, stepped away and began to imperceptibly move toward her.

Clementine realized it was the man who had been carrying the baby ocelot. That probably meant the three smugglers had not managed to make a clean getaway, and the animals could still be retrieved from the truck.

"Stop right there," she ordered coldly.

The smuggler smiled insolently, confidently.

"You won't shoot, lady. You don't want to harm an unarmed man."

"Those babies you and your partners were stealing were also unarmed and helpless, you creep," she said in a quiet, deadly tone. "If you don't want a bullet in your kneecap, you'd better quit while you're ahead."

The man halted, uncertain, and Preston, no longer able to contain himself, whirled and put him out of commission with a solid left hook.

The thug who'd been beating the stuffing out of Preston tried to run, but Preston tackled him, and gave him a taste of his own medicine before sending him to oblivion.

"Good job," Clementine said appreciatively.

"I do better one on one," Preston told her modestly.

"I can testify to that," she said, smiling.

The man on the floor started to regain consciousness, and managed to stand up.

Preston swiftly closed the distance between them, and grabbing the man's shirt, propped him up against the wall, and then punched his lights out.

Rubbing his hands together, Preston said, "Now, where were we?"

Suddenly sirens blared in the distance, and Preston asked, "Cops?"

"I got a keeper to call them. It appears that although the local law enforcement is underpaid, overworked and sometimes less than competent, they were not part of Ronald's outfit."

"And Ronald?"

"He's safely tied up and will be picked up by the police momentarily," Clementine told him, putting her gun away. She was always glad when she was not forced to fire her weapon. While not afraid to use it, Clementine believed that one should try to resolve conflicts through logic and compromise first.

"Is it safe to approach you now?" Preston asked, amusement threading his voice.

Clementine raised her hands. "Totally unarmed and harmless."

"You'll *never* be that, oh my darling, darling Clementine," Preston told her in a voice thick with desire.

"You just couldn't resist, could you?" Clementine smiled, shaking her head.

"You have to admit, I've shown admirable restraint and self-control up to now," he murmured.

"Control comes in handy sometimes," she said, raising her hands and running them through his hair. "But restraint—I believe we can do without that for a while."

"Hey, lovebirds, remember me? Think you can wait on the foreplay until I'm untied?"

Seventeen

While one of the veterinarians tended to Ford's cuts and bruises, he explained what had happened to him and insisted he did not have to be flown to a mainland hospital.

Ronald had indeed been the mastermind behind both the smuggling and blackmailing operations. Through his connections in the States, he would find out which high-profile businessman could least afford to be implicated in a drug scandal. But Ronald was not too selective. It did not matter to him whether they were indeed users or had other secrets which could be unearthed if word got out that they were involved in drugs, or their position in the community was such that no hint of impropriety would be tolerated: he was an equal-opportunity extortionist.

Of course, he could not keep the scam alive for too long. Already, rumblings had started in the business community when a physician and pharmaceuticals supplier had compared notes. It would only have been a matter of time before this part of the operation was uncovered, and the police contacted on Isla Gaucha to start an investigation.

In the meantime, Ronald Beinor had another venture going…he was nothing if not versatile. He smuggled hard-to-get animals—animals that were in high demand precisely because they were so rare, or on the verge of becoming extinct. Ronald would sell them to unscrupulous zoos or private collectors. He also provided anything else that was marketable, like leather, fur, skins, ivory.

Ford had overheard that Ronald hoped to retire within the next couple of years, and had planned to do so with Celeste. Her request for a divorce had caught him by surprise, and so he had speeded up the proceedings, planning on one last giant job.

Ronald had originally tried to dissuade Celeste from divorcing him, and when she would not listen to his pleas, he had tried to persuade her not to go to Isla Gaucha. When that request had also failed, he'd planned on going through with the divorce, hoping to win her back afterward.

Once Clementine entered into the picture, along with an investigative reporter, he had been forced to drastically change his plans again. He had no compunction in killing rival Ford, nor his nephew. And when Clementine would not back off, he'd felt he had no recourse but to get rid of her, too. He'd figured that would drive Celeste back into his arms. The shock and tragic loss of her beloved child would put Celeste in a very vulnerable position, and Ronald had felt confident that with his constant attention, he would be able to keep her at his side.

Clementine was still not able to reconcile the image of a man who could love a woman so much with that of someone who showed no scruples about killing anyone in his way, who evinced no remorse about extorting money, who had no regard for nature and its fragile creatures.

Ronald had indeed been a brilliant, complex man.

And as Preston had mentioned, and she'd discovered in her business, very few people—even those who broke the law with regularity—were either totally good or bad. Even the worst of the human race usually possessed the capacity to love something, or someone.

And Celeste was an easy person to love.

When the vet was done, Ford declared himself fit to travel. He asked Preston, "Has Delores made an appearance yet?"

"Luckily, yes," Preston said, grinning. "A belated one, due to a last-minute shopping spree."

"That'll be my divorce present to her—aside from a generous settlement," Ford said, unperturbed. "Spendthrift or not, Delores was always a lot of fun, and I know that, in her own way, she cared for me."

Clementine reflected that Ford was also an easy person to love.

"Ford, I'm afraid I owe you an apology...."

"Don't worry about it, my dear. You were right to feel suspicious, given the facts at hand. And had I listened to my nephew, and his *own* suspicions, you would not have been forced to rescue me."

"But I shouldn't have suspected you," Clementine said, contrite. "I wasted all that time and energy distrusting you."

Ford patted her hand consolingly. "You were keeping your options open, and even went against every instinct in considering Preston's charges, who, by the way, had his own doubts about you." Clementine's narrowed gaze flew to Preston, who looked uncomfortable at Ford's bringing the touchy subject up. "I guess both of you, employing sound investigative procedure, even checked each other out, didn't you?" Clementine blushed and Preston looked even more uncomfortable, knowing his uncle was giving "checking out" added meaning. Ford, blue eyes twinkling, added, "Besides, it's not easy to distrust family—and Beinor was that, even if only through marriage."

"No longer, thank God." Clementine shook her head with distaste, and Preston and Ford laughed.

"Speaking of family," Ford began, getting up slowly and leaning against Preston for a minute before straightening to his full height.

"Are you sure you're all right?" Preston asked, concerned.

"There's bound to be a doctor at the resort. Why don't I call ahead?" Clementine suggested.

"I'll be all right with some rest and good food," Ford said, waving away their concerns. "Would you mind, Clemmie, if I call on your mother—once my own divorce to Delores is final?"

"Thanks for asking, but Celeste makes up her own mind."

"I would like to know *your* opinion, my dear," Ford told her gravely.

Clementine looked from uncle to nephew, and marveled at how close she had become to the two men in such a short period of time. The old adage was true: danger did compress and intensify emotion.

She told Ford, "In my opinion, you and my mother make a wonderful couple."

"Thank you, Clemmie," Ford said. "I will never attempt to take your father's place, but it's nice to know that I have your blessing."

He began walking toward a police car. "Well, if you're done here, how about joining Delores, Celeste and me for dinner tonight? The police have agreed to wait on our statements until tomorrow."

"That should be quite a threesome," Preston said, amused.

"It's too late to get a divorce today—besides, I'd like to be able to move at a pace faster than a shuffle for the momentous occasion—but I still want to spend the evening with Celeste."

Massaging a back sore and stiff from being tied up for so long, Ford added ruefully, "Having been rescued and given a new lease on life, I want to share every minute of it with Celeste."

"If you don't mind, Uncle, Clementine and I have some things to finish up."

"Oh?" Ford asked.

"I promised Clem I'd help clean up the mess we started in the compound. Also, we need to collect our mountain-climbing equipment so we can turn it in at the rental office."

"Didn't know you to be so civic-minded, nephew," Ford said, grinning.

Preston presented an innocent face that fooled no one.

"Can I at least count on you two being at the divorce ceremony tomorrow?"

"Wild horses couldn't keep me away from seeing the fair Delores depart," Preston said.

Ford laughed.

"Don't take too long...um...finding your equipment," Ford told Preston before informing a policeman he was ready to go back to the resort.

"Since we've already turned in the equipment we rented, what exactly are we collecting?" Clementine asked as she and Preston watched Ford climb into the black police car.

"How about some memories?" he told her, pulling her against him.

The roaring of the waterfall, the scent of wild orchids and Preston's touch overwhelmed Clementine's senses.

"Aren't you afraid of leeches anymore?" Clementine asked him, trying to recover her breath and sanity. "You seem very popular with the fauna on this island."

"With you to protect me, there's nothing for me to fear," Preston murmured against her lips.

His fingertips traced the curve of her shoulder, slid down her arm and then descended to cup her heart-shaped derriere and press her closer.

Clementine's hands caressed his biceps, then moved upward to his sculpted shoulders. Digging her fingers into his hair, she reveled in the silky softness of its damp waves.

Preston dropped to his knees in the shallow water of the pool, and his mouth roamed the flesh of her stomach before moving up to swallow a breast with his lips. He suckled the nipple, hard and deep, and Clementine felt her bones dissolve. His teeth nipped the hardened buds, and she felt a deep, hot wetness start in the center of her body.

Preston's tongue traced a direct, downward line, into her belly button, out, curling into the auburn thicket at the juncture of her thighs, and then inside.

Throwing her head back, Clementine bit her lips to contain the moan that erupted from deep within her.

As Preston's hands left her buttocks and opened her to him more fully, she put her hands on his head, trying to stop the tortuous ecstasy.

But Preston would not desist. Tongue and teeth joined in a maddening combination that had Clementine disintegrating into mindless, shapeless oblivion.

When her knees buckled, he caught her, curved her legs around his hips, and rose with her.

His eyes shot silver sparks, and his expression mirrored the intensity of emotion when he told her, "I love you, Clem."

She responded, "I love you, Preston," as he entered her.

Half in, half out of the water, Clementine wrapped her thighs even more tightly around his lean hips, and held on as he pierced her, withdrew, then pierced her again, the unbearable friction soul-destroying.

As Preston's rocking motion grew even more unrestrained, she nipped at his shoulder, and one of her nails scratched a nipple that instantly stood at attention.

Preston covered her laughing lips with his, and as she began to climax again, his tongue stabbed her mouth and engaged hers in a mirror image of his bucking hips.

Feeling the heat of the afternoon sun on her back, the velvety hardness of Preston's chest against her breasts, and the cold water slapping against her legs and hips, Clementine thought she would explode, and never be whole again.

But Preston held on to her, and as they reached the pinnacle together, so, too, did they make their peaceful descent in harmony.

Grabbing on to his shoulders, Clementine placed little love bites on his neck. "Do you think we could do this on a sane, stable surface for once?"

"And lose our spontaneity and excitement?"

Her hand found him, and within seconds, his erection grew by leaps and bounds. Feeling his slick, engorged organ pulsate within her grasp, she asked, "Do you really think we can't recapture this on a comfy, soft bed?" she asked, stroking him into throbbing, feverish hardness.

"You've got a point," Preston told her, his voice thick with passion. After a pause, he repositioned her, and, her legs circling his waist, penetrated her in one swift, hard motion.

"Should we wait until we get back to the resort?" he asked wickedly.

"Naughty boy," Clementine scolded, slapping one beautifully shaped buttock sharply. "It's not nice to tease."

Her legs gripped him and held him, and her internal muscles worked to drive him deeper into her.

Preston groaned, his face flushed with screaming urgency.

He began pumping wildly, uncontrollably, while she held on for the ride with all her might, and massaged him internally with all her strength.

They called out each other's names as they came simultaneously, and the ardent sounds were carried on perfumed breezes, and mingled with the happy cries of countless birds.

"You are looking marvelous, Clemmie," Celeste told Clementine the following day as Ford bade goodbye to Delores.

Having met young, beautiful, effervescent Delores, Clementine could see how Ford could have been attracted to the woman. But her youthful blond looks—as well as personality and depth—could not compare with Celeste's.

Looking pointedly at Preston's arm, which seemed permanently attached to her daughter, Celeste said innocently, "It seems this little vacation has revitalized you. Or is it the exotic, erotic appeal of the island?"

"Mother, just because you can't get embarrassed does not mean you have the right to make others uncomfortable," Clementine told her.

"Embarrassed, Tweetie?" Smiling at Ford, who leaned down to place an affectionate kiss on Celeste's smooth cheek, Celeste asked him, "Don't you think the appropriate words are *positively glowing,* Ford?"

"Now that you mention it, even Preston seems to fairly—*sparkle.* Is that the right word?"

"More like *satisfied,* wouldn't you say?" Celeste offered, unrepentant.

"All right, Mother," Clementine said, resigned.

"I wouldn't talk, Uncle," Preston said, aiming for a severe tone but failing when he saw the loving look Ford gave Celeste.

"Will you be joining us for dinner tonight?" Celeste asked.

Before Clementine could answer, Preston spoke up. "Actually, Clem and I were planning on a private celebration of our own."

"Want to meet us for drinks first, or dancing later?"

"I don't think we'll have the time, Uncle," Preston told Ford.

"Why not?" Celeste asked.

"Clem is anxious to try out the beds of the resort."

"Preston!" Clementine scolded him. Knowing she was turning several shades of red, she told Celeste and Ford, "I think Preston can wait to try out the mattresses. I wouldn't miss your celebration—especially the dancing after dinner."

Preston blanched. "Please, anything but dancing!"

"That'll teach you not to embarrass me," Clementine told Preston sternly.

Gathering Clementine in his arms, Preston said, "You have a whole lifetime in which to punish me. Just promise me to never, ever be gentle."

As Celeste and Ford looked on, arms around each other, Clementine locked her hands behind Preston's neck, and said, "Before these interested witnesses, Preston, you've got my solemn oath."

* * * * *

Get Ready to be Swept Away by
Silhouette's Spring Collection

Abduction
Seduction

These passion-filled stories explore both the dangerous
desires of men and the seductive powers of women.
Written by three of our most celebrated authors, they are
sure to capture your hearts.

Diana Palmer
Brings us a spin-off of her Long, Tall Texans series

Joan Johnston
Crafts a beguiling Western romance

Rebecca Brandewyne
New York Times bestselling author
makes a smashing contemporary debut

Available in March at your favorite retail outlet.

Bestselling Author

Elise Title

Anything less than everything is not enough.

Coming in January 1995, Sylver Cassidy and Kate Paley take
on the movers and shakers of Hollywood. Young, beautiful,
been-there, done-it-all type women, they're ready to live by their
own rules and stand by their own mistakes. With love on the
horizon, can two women bitten by the movie bug really have it
all? Find out in

HOT PROPERTY

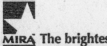

MONTANA Mavericks™

Stories that capture living and loving beneath the Big Sky, where legends live on...and mystery lingers.

This January, the intrigue continues with

OUTLAW LOVERS
by Pat Warren

He was a wanted man. She was the beckoning angel who offered him a hideout. Now their budding passion has put them both in danger. And he'd do anything to protect her.

Don't miss a minute of the loving as the passion continues with:

WAY OF THE WOLF
by Rebecca Daniels (February)

THE LAW IS NO LADY
by Helen R. Myers (March)

FATHER FOUND
by Laurie Paige (April)
and many more!

Only from ▼ Silhouette® where passion lives.

New York Times **Bestselling Author**

Jayne Ann Krentz

Can a business arrangement become a marriage?
Find out this January with

Test of Time

He wanted a business partner. She wanted a partner to
love. There was hard work ahead to win both his trust
and his heart. She had to show him that there was more
to this business deal than simply saying, *"I do."*

Do they stand a chance at making the *only* reason the
real reason to share a lifetime?

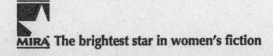

MIRA The brightest star in women's fiction

MJAKTOT

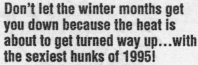

Beginning next month from

SILHOUETTE®

Desire®

FROM HERE TO MATERNITY

by Elizabeth Bevarly

A new series celebrating the unexpected joys of motherhood—and fatherhood!

Three single women each meet the man of their dreams...and receive a precious surprise package from a certain stork.

In February—
A DAD LIKE DANIEL (#908)

In April—
THE PERFECT FATHER (#920)

In June—
DR. DADDY (#933)

Watch these soon-to-be moms as they are swept off their feet and into the maternity ward!
Only from Silhouette Desire.

Robert...Luke...Noah
Three proud, strong brothers who live—and
love—by

THE CODE OF THE WEST

Meet the Tanner man, starting with
Silhouette Desire's *Man of the Month* for
February, Robert Tanner, in Anne McAllister's

COWBOYS DON'T CRY

Robert Tanner never let any woman get close
to him—especially not Maggie MacLeod. But
the tempting new owner of his ranch was
determined to get past the well-built defenses
around his heart....

And be sure to watch for brothers Luke and Noah,
in their own stories, COWBOYS DON'T QUIT
and COWBOYS DON'T STAY, throughout 1995!

Only from